Altered

A Devoured Novel

Book Three

Shelly Crane

Author and publisher do not have control of and do not assume responsibility for third party websites and their content.

Cover design by MaelDesign
Editing services provided by Todd Barselow

Printed in the USA

1 2 3 4 5 6 7 8 9 10

Paperback available, also in eBook formats through Amazon, CreateSpace, Barnes & Noble, Apple, Kobo, and wherever books are sold.

More information can be found at the author's website:

http://shellycrane.blogspot.com

ISBN-13: 978-1499602395
ISBN-10: 1499602391

For Axel.

These past two years have been anything but easy. When we said 'til death do us part' you never imagined that this was what you were signing up for, did you? But these past couple years have been such a blessing, too. I never have to wonder if dinner will be taken care of, or if the kids have brushed their teeth, or just if…everything will be okay.

Thank you for that.

We don't know what will happen in the years to come, I know that, but I know that you'll be there, and nothing is more amazing than knowing that the one person I love most in the world is the one person who loves me back. Thank you for being you, for getting me, for being sarcastic, for being willing to do what needs to be done. When it's your turn, I'll be there.

I love you more.

You know when you're on a course that you know is the right one. *You can't explain it, you can't define it,* you don't know how you got there or what *all the obstacles will be, you just know the end result will* be **amazing** and it will be **worth** it?

That's the road I'm on.

Full speed ahead, no blinkers or turn signals. **Just cruise control.**

-Fay

Prologue

I stood there and watched as he married Clara, as he turned away from everything that we stood for and became human in every way possible. And somehow he was dragging me down with him. I was changing, I could feel it. Ever since that human had gotten her claws in my brother and bonded to him, I had begun to change, too—though I'd never admit that to anyone.

I stood there and watched as she looked up at him and I knew she loved him. I wanted to be happy for him—I came back for his wedding for God's sakes—but that was the problem wasn't it? I wasn't supposed to be happy for him. I wasn't supposed to want to see him get married or anything else. This whole thing was making me soft. I *hated* that I cared. Though the bond wasn't there anymore, there was still a lingering in the back of my mind that made me wonder how they were doing.

And it pissed me right off.

As soon as they said I do and he took her in his human arms, holding her and kissing her, I stormed down the aisle. I'd done my brotherly duty, hadn't I? I was done with this charade of human bullcrap. So done. I got into the car that I'd hotwired and went back into town. I went into the first bar I saw and dared anyone to look at me except the one person I was after.

The brunette in the corner would work just fine. She favored Clara a bit and I smiled at the satisfaction that was going to give me. She was standing by the jukebox looking through the songs with a beer in her hand. I stalked up behind her slowly and let my eyes roam the selection as I let my thighs press against the back of hers. Her breath swept from her lips in a hiss. She turned to put me in my place, but immediately lost her train of thought when our gazes collided. Her lips fell open, but it wasn't to reprimand me for my behavior. Her eyes moved to my lips and back up again. I felt them form into a grin. Ah, so good to be bad again.

"Hi."

"Hi," she returned, no voice, just breath.

"Find anything good?" Her eyes widened a little. "On the jukebox."

"Oh," she said and turned back, snapping out of the trance finally. She cleared her throat and clutched her beer bottle to her chest like a security blanket. "Not yet. Nice accent."

"Thanks. Mind if I...?" I pointed and leaned in to see the song titles.

"Find something to dance to," she ordered.

I looked over and knew this was in the bag. I didn't need to feed the meter on this deal any longer. She was practically salivating as her hips swayed before I'd even put the quarter in the jukebox. I took her arm in my hand and leaned in. "I'd rather go somewhere, if I'm being honest. Just you and me."

"Ok," she couldn't say quickly enough. "My place is—"

"Too far." My hands gripping those hips tightly, I pushed her out the back door to the dark spot I knew would be there. I let the door slam behind me and turned her to face me, pressing her back to the wall. Her dazed eyes tried to focus on mine. I smiled inside—and I hadn't even started yet. This was too easy. "Right here is just fine."

"But, someone might come back here."

"No one will come," I assured her, pushing my persuasion into every word. "And if they do, I'll bloody well take care of them. But what I really want is to take care of you."

I opened my senses up, wide open, and let my nose coast across her cheek to her ear. Her fingers gripped my shirt and her breath caught. I could taste her lust all over my tongue and all I wanted was to drown in it. I smiled and let my lips touch her skin. "What's your name?"

"Isabella."

I rolled my eyes. "Isabella. What a sweet name. Do you taste as sweet as you sound?"

She smiled, almost shyly. "You are awfully good at that."

"What?"

"Making me feel like you actually want me for more than just a good time."

I paused and looked at her eyes. Green. Like Clara's. My God…I was ruined, wasn't I? She smiled again and rubbed my chest.

"Don't worry, slick. I'm not about to go all *Wicker Park* on you. I was just saying that it's obvious you've had some practice at this." Her smile was genuine. It wasn't a sloppy, come-hither look they usually are when women in places like this try to get with a man. It was so completely genuine. It enraged me in my soul that I noticed this, let alone cared.

I didn't say anything else, I just moved in, letting my lips touch hers. The harder I pressed, the more she fed me. My eyes rolled back into my head at having my first good meal in days. The more clothes disappeared, the more I felt like my true self was coming back, the more *evil* I felt.

When it was all over and we dressed, I started to walk away without a word, but she asked me for my name. I let it build slowly. I wanted to feel like the Devourer I knew I was so I unleashed the terror on her, seeing her eyes search around and the way she skittered into the back wall and covered her face with nowhere else to go.

And I fed.

I fed on her terror and fright and it tasted like heaven in my mouth. But as I looked down at that woman who had just given herself to me, and I hadn't even had to persuade her to, it washed over me all at once how I didn't really want to hurt her. That I wanted to hurt *people*, but not her. Not really. I had gotten everything I needed from her without doing that, hadn't I? I was full and sated. Now I was just letting my true nature take over, letting the devourer in me come out and play.

But wasn't that what I was supposed to do? I looked down at that woman and was so confused. I cursed Clara and Eli and all their love and human bullcrap for turning me into the thing that I was now.

No. I realized then that this was my turning point. That if I let this girl go, that I would be just like my brother one day and that wasn't what I wanted. I was not going to be some human. I was a devourer. My chin ached from clenching it so tightly. I turned my glare fully on her and knew that honestly it wasn't her fault, but she was about to pay the price for my brother's mistake.

"I'm sorry, love." I lifted her by her arms and then leaned into her, pressing her to the wall.

"For what?" her small voice asked, falsely reassured by my about-face. "What are you doing to me?"

"I'm sorry that our night is just beginning."

She seemed to understand and her face crumpled. "Please. I'm sorry for whatever I said to—"

"It's not you," I told her and grinned as evilly as I could muster, "it's me."

One
Fay

"Fay Hopkins."

I rose slowly and stood, looking at the judge, awaiting my fate. I prayed his next words showed me mercy that I myself hadn't bestowed upon anyone in the last year. I had been bitter and angry, and no one was safe from my wrath. Especially not Clara. I closed my eyes as I remembered all the things I'd said to her.

"Miss Hopkins, it is the decision of this court that you be dishonorably discharged for your actions on…"

I tuned out the rest, but got the gist. Oh…what was I going to do now? I had nowhere to go. The military was all I had. Pastor and Mrs. Ruth weren't my family like they were Clara's. I barely knew them. Clara had run off and married some idiot boy and they moved. I had her last letter. I'm sure she thought I never kept them, but I did.

I had no choice but to eat a ton of crow and go find her. Who knew—she may not even want me now. I may have waited too long. I *was* really angry with her. I mean, I still was. She did get the easy street in all this and then wanted me to put Band-Aids on everything like when we were little and make everything better. But she was too naïve to see that everything wasn't going to be better.

And I was young, too. It wasn't my responsibility to deal with.

The judge's gavel banging made me jump and he glared at me for daydreaming. "I see even now that nothing gets through to you. You're dismissed. I hope once you get home and are surrounded by people you know and are used to that it can help you to see that the world isn't out to get you, Miss Hopkins. The world is actually a pretty fair place."

I felt the scoff rising from my soul. "Not from where I stand."

I turned, grabbing my bag, and left without a backward look.

———

My Jetta made it about a hundred miles past the Montana state line before the engine gave out. I was almost completely out of cash, hadn't slept properly in days, hadn't eaten a real meal that wasn't from a gas station in I didn't know how long. I left my car smoking on the side of road and shook my head as I headed across the street to the motel. The difference between a motel and a hotel was night and day in small towns like this. It could mean the difference between getting sliced in the middle of the night, but it was all that I could see.

I prayed—again with the praying, like someone was listening—that there was a room for less than thirty dollars. Otherwise, I was screwed. Because I only had thirty-five dollars to my name and that five dollars was my dinner for the night. Tomorrow would have to worry about itself.

A car honked as it barely missed me, skidding past on the road behind me. I didn't even know what town I was in. I just knew I was close to Clara. I opened the door, the chime of the doorbell and the smell of muck and cigarettes slamming into me. I coughed, offending the young attendant. He scowled at me and cocked his head. "Can I help you, duchess?"

"Do you have a room, please?" I asked in my most pleading, small voice.

He thought, pausing. "For the night or for the week?"

"Just for the night."

"Working girl?" He smiled. I tried not to cringe.

"No. Just traveling through on my way to see my sister."

His look of interest went away and so did my hope of getting a room. "Seventy-nine plus tax."

"Please…is there anything cheaper than that?"

"You can take the room or get out of here. I ain't running a charity."

I sighed and turned to go. I could sleep in my car, I just didn't want to. As soon as I got inside, I tried to lock the doors, but my battery was dead. The automatic doors locks wouldn't work; nothing did, with the battery dead. I sighed again and laughed. It turned hysterical as I laid my head on the steering wheel.

Nothing was working out for me anymore. Nothing. The world was giving me the big middle finger. I deserved it. I leaned back and hoped that no one messed with me while I slept. I couldn't even lay my seat back because the seat was powered. So I sat there and closed my eyes, trying to forget my mess of a life for a moment so I could sleep.

Eventually, I did sleep. I dreamt someone was touching me. I moved my face toward his hand and he chuckled. That seemed to wake me and I opened my eyes to find the motel attendant crouching down next to me with my car door open. I opened my mouth, but before I could scream or say anything, he covered it roughly with his hand. I could tell my eyes were as wide as tangerines. He smiled at me and said softly, "It's okay. I'm not going to hurt you."

I scoffed beneath his hand and his smile widened. He gripped my arm and tugged me out of my car and pressed me to the side of it.

"I'll give you a place to stay for the night. No charge. You give me a little something in return, okay?" I shook my head hard under his hand and he gripped me to stop it. "No harm, no foul. You need a place to stay and I like you. What's the problem?" I mumbled under his palm. He laughed a little. "No screaming, beautiful."

My skin literally crawled under my clothes as he let his hand slide from my mouth to my neck. "I said I'm not into that kind of thing. I'm fine in my car, but thanks."

I waited, my breath pulling from my lungs painfully.

"Ah, honey," he drawled and I knew it was over, "this isn't a negotiation."

I turned to run, but he had a handful of my hair before I could get anywhere. I used my elbow to his gut and he '*oophed*', which just upset him more. He was a lot bigger than me. He opened the backdoor of my car and tried to shove me in. I knew if he got me in there, I wasn't coming back out. So I fought as hard as I could, used every bit of training I could recall, but honestly, I'd done basic training and that was it. People thought just because you were in the military that you were some kind of killing machine. That's not what it meant at all.

When I got a good palm jab to his nose, he cursed and that was it for me. Any bit of gentleness he'd been reserving for me was gone. He held my arm behind my back and yanked the handful of hair in his fist so tight that I saw stars. "You little b—"

"What have we here?"

We both turned to look at the man who was standing near the back of the car. He had an accent and looked like death warmed over. He was pale and disheveled; his hair was a mess and his clothes wrinkled and dirty. He stared at me, his mouth open, and though he seemed to be trying to help me, he also seemed to be enraptured and licked his lip more than once as he looked between the man and me.

"None of your business," the man barked. "Scram."

The interrupter looked at me and watched. His eyes...were purple. I could see that even in the darkness. He licked his bottom lip again, but gave me an almost sad look as he began to back away. A sob escaped my throat at the fact that I'd never reach Clara, never get to tell her that I was sorry, that I'd been wrong to blame her just because I happened to be older when our parents died. Of course I'd been given more responsibility. Of course people were going to expect more from me. But she'd never know that I loved her. She'd never know.

Another sob rose when my captor actually chuckled, realizing that my rescuer wasn't rescuing me at all, but was backing away. I had nothing left to hold back for, so I let is all go. It bubbled up and my chest ached so hard. The guy who had interrupted us gasped and looked at me over his shoulder, his eyes lidded, and he swayed. I was so confused as to what was going on, but it didn't matter. He wasn't helping me and the man wasn't waiting any longer. He turned to put me in the car. I started to fight, but no matter how hard I fought, he was overpowering me. He raised his arm back, slapping my cheek and then slamming his fist into my gut when I kept fighting. I could barely breathe through the pain as I gagged and gasped. That effectively ended all movement from me.

"Now, stop fighting me," he growled and pushed me back into the car, lifting my legs. "I'm actually a good guy once you get to know me."

Then he was gone. I gasped at the sudden movement and clasped my stomach, finally able to breathe and get some relief. The interrupter stood there, one arm outstretched into the air, which he'd slung the man off with.

"I somehow doubt that," he said, his voice grating.

He fell to his knees, looking worse than I did somehow. I looked between the two of them, one way across the road sprawled on the sidewalk, and one on his knees as he held on to his last bit of alertness. He swayed and stared up at me. "If you want to wait for him to wake up, then that's fine, but I suggest that we go."

"We?" I breathed.

"I don't think it's a secret that I'm not exactly…doing so hot." He swayed again, catching himself on his fist in the dirt. I moved forward to put my hands on his shoulders to help steady him. "Where are you staying tonight? Your car's done for," he stated the ever-so-obvious.

"I didn't have enough for a room," I told him softly. I leaned down to look at his face. "I was sleeping in my car."

"Help me up."

Under normal circumstances, I would have told him to go to hell, but he had just saved me and he was obviously distressed himself…to some degree. I didn't know what was wrong with him, but I couldn't walk away after he'd helped me. I pulled on his arm until he was standing over me. He looked down at me, seeming to study me. He looked like he was starving. He took the ends of my hair in between his fingers and rubbed it for a few seconds before letting it fall.

"I need something from you."

I sighed, my hope falling all over again. "I'm not having sex with you—"

"Not that. Come on. I'll get us a room."

"I'm not…"

He started to turn. "I need you to help me. I haven't fed in so long. I'm weak. Get me to the motel room. I'll get you dinner and a place to stay if you'll just help me without question."

I stalled. He hadn't fed? That was a weird way to say he hadn't eaten. He growled. Actually growled. "Why would I save you only to hurt you myself?" Good point. "Besides, I can barely walk. I'm not going to be of any use to a woman tonight." He grinned devilishly and I knew that when he was at his best, all cleaned up and on his game, he was a force to be reckoned with. "You're safe...for now."

I sighed, biting my lip and knowing that this was my only chance at getting to see Clara again.

"Fine." I leaned down and put my shoulder under his arm and helped pull him up. I looked over to see my attacker still out cold on the pavement. But his breath puffed in the chilled night air, so I knew he was alive. I shook my head and looked over at the man I was holding. I hadn't realized how tall he was, or how close he was. I tried to move back some but there was nowhere to go unless I let him go. I sighed, my puff of breath meeting his in the small space between us as he stared down at me. He seemed puzzled by something. Almost an angry puzzlement, like he was fascinated and couldn't stop, but didn't like what he was finding.

"Let's get a room, blue eyes."

"Fay," I said and gulped at how affected it sounded. I coughed and hoisted him up a little as I started to help him across the street. "And if you think I'm sleeping in the same bed with you—"

"I don't sleep. I just need to rest. The chair will do just fine."

"You don't sleep," I drawled and didn't believe a word of it. "You look as if you could keel over at any minute, buddy."

"As soon as I feed, I'll be fine."

"Then let's eat first," I insisted because I was starving and if he was offering up a free meal, I was taking. Though by the looks of him, I didn't know how he was doing so badly if he had the means and money to take care of himself. Why not just go eat if he was so hungry? "Let's grab something quick at the diner at the motel. That okay with you?"

"Whatever, blue eyes," he grumbled and closed his eyes as he let me guide him. When we came to the diner's door, a mother and her child were coming out. The little girl was crying about something, obviously upset. The mom was coddling her in an amused but exasperated way that showed she'd been at it for a while. "You can't only eat pie for dinner. It doesn't work that way, Carline."

I snorted. That's why she was so mad—her mother saddled that precious little thing with a name like Carline. I sympathized. Fay wasn't exactly a young name, and then when you added my middle name Annie to the mix, I was doomed to hick nickname hell. Fay Annie Hopkins. I'd been picked on a lot for it. Fannie…Ah, how I hated that nickname. Clara and my parents especially let that stick and wouldn't let it go no matter how much I said I hated it.

Now…I'd give anything to hear Clara call me Fannie. Maybe not. I'd never felt this hopeless in my entire life. Even though I knew where she was, I felt like she was drifting further and further away and I'd never catch up to her. I didn't know if she was safe or happy or…

My rescuer sucked in a breath beside me and I looked over to see his eyes now open. He watched me, his mouth slightly open. His tongue snaked out to taste his bottom lip, but he grimaced. "Oh, gah… What are you thinking about?"

I felt my brows gravitate toward each other in confusion. "What?"

"You're…you're sad. I can see it. What are thinking about?"

Before I could answer, the little girl bumped into his leg. She looked up at him like he had dropped her lollipop. "I'm sorry," the mother said, but chuckled and took the daughter's hand. "Carline, say you're sorry."

"Sorry, *sir*," the little girl, who couldn't be more than four, spouted sarcastically.

They walked away and the man stood there, his mouth open, and watched them go. Then he broke into the biggest smile. His chest began to shake and he looked up at the sky, shaking his head. "Eli, you bastard. I bet you're just loving this, aren't you?"

His words were harsh, but he was still smiling. I was confused, but he was obviously having some revelation. I waited and eventually he looked back over and down at me. "Ready to eat, blue eyes?"

"Uh…are you in need of some medication or…"

He laughed hard. "Ah, man. We are going to get along so well. Come on." He tugged me into the diner. Or dragged me really because he could barely hold himself up. He slammed into a booth and I slid into the seat across from him. The diner was clean for all intents and purposes, but would be receiving no awards for service or cuisine. I could easily see that from where we sat.

As the middle-aged woman waddled over and asked what we wanted to drink, he waved her off and said he didn't want anything. I looked blankly at him. "I thought you were so hungry. What do you mean you don't want anything?"

He seemed to think about that and then grimaced. "Oh, yeah. Bollocks." I scoffed, but he smiled at her and began his list.

"I'll take the strongest coffee you've got, a stack of flapjacks, and a side of bacon—enough pig to feed a small army."

"So a lot of bacon, then," she drawled sarcastically.

"You went to Harvard, I see."

"And I'll take," I rushed on and scanned the menu quickly for something, "the same, minus the arsenal of bacon. A regular ol' portion of bacon is fine."

She left without another word and I looked over at him. "Me Fay, you…?"

"Enoch." He smiled. "At your service."

"Enoch." I smiled back. I couldn't help myself. "I really like that." His purple eyes met mine and he seemed again like he was trying to figure some puzzle out. "What do you do?"

"Professional traveler."

"A Gypsy?"

He barked a laugh. "No, not really," he evaded. "What do you do?"

I let my eyes fall to the table. He sucked in a quick breath like he was in pain. I looked up at him and he was watching me with his mouth open. He licked his lip and shook his head. "Ok, don't tell me right now. Right now, I need to feed."

"She'll bring the food soon. Besides, you didn't even want to eat, remember," I reminded him.

He nodded carefully. "This is where the part about you helping me comes in. When we finish our meal, I'll let you know what we need to do, all right." It wasn't a question. He brightened and looked over at the door as it chimed. "Never mind. I think dinner just walked in."

I glanced over, feeling more creeped out by the second, and saw a man and woman—obviously in a fight. They hissed in whispers and glared at each other as they found a seat. I looked back at Enoch, so happy to finally know his name, but so confused. I smirked, willing to play his game if that was what he needed right now.

"So you're a vampire or something?" He chuckled and shook his head, staring at the table as I went on. "You want me to club them over the head when they leave so you can suck them dry in the parking lot. That wasn't exactly what I signed up for in my part of this arrangement."

"No," he said softly and looked up at me. When he saw my face, how that smile seemed to affect me, his face hardened a little. "No," he said harder. "It's nothing like that. Just forget I brought it up. It's been taken care of." He leaned back and watched the couple, his lips slightly open.

Their waitress came and took their order and they seemed to fight about that, too. Enoch's eyes closed and he sighed. I wanted to bolt, but something was holding me back. Something was keeping me there. "Are you all right?"

"I'm fine, blue eyes," he said, never opening his eyes. But when a chair scraped, we both looked over to see the couple storming out. "Bloody hell," he muttered. "Should've known it wouldn't be that easy."

"What's going on with you?" I asked quietly. Maybe he escaped from somewhere, a clinic or an asylum or something. Maybe there was some medication he hadn't taken but really should have. I didn't know, but the guy clearly had something going on upstairs.

He looked at me sadly and I didn't understand why. "We'll talk about it later. You can tell me about your job," he said slowly and nudged my foot with his gently. "Anything you want to talk about."

"I shouldn't tell you all my secrets. You're a stranger," I said to lighten the mood. "Haven't you ever heard of stranger danger?"

He grinned—that grin transforming his whole face. "They coined that term because of me, sweetheart."

Two
Enoch

It had been exactly thirty-two days since I had forced an emotional feed from someone. I followed people around until I found someone who was pissed off or sad and then I fed. It had been like this for months now. It didn't always work out and sometimes I had to cave and force my terror on them because I was about to starve, but mostly, I avoided it at all costs.

Ever since that night in the alley after Eli and Clara's wedding, my life hadn't been the same. I couldn't get that woman's screams out of my head. I dreamed about them—as much as a devourer can dream because we don't sleep. They invaded my thoughts during the day in flashes that came out of nowhere. I got no peace, no rest. I tried everything to rid myself of it. At first, I ignored it and went on with life, but soon realized that that just made it worse. When I stopped bringing terror to others, it got better.

Like I was being punished.

It didn't go away, but she doesn't haunt me as badly anymore. I've done everything I can to make up for what I did to her in the alley that day by almost starving myself. But it's a miserable existence. It's a pointless existence.

I've thought about finding Eli and seeing what he thinks about what's going on, but I knew he would just say I was becoming like him. The change in him began with a little boy and a revolving door. After that, he didn't force feed on people unless he had to either, but he hadn't gone to my extreme. I would literally bring myself to the brink of starvation. He said he found a way around it by going to high school. That there was enough angst and drama there that he never had to force fear on anyone, but I wasn't doing *that*. I'd live this miserable existence if that's what it took, but I wasn't going to high school and have some love sick girl fall in love with me.

No.

I looked up at find Fay watching me. I sighed and looked away. If I couldn't get her to talk about whatever made her so upset earlier, then I was going to have to force it out of her. I was too far gone. This was the brink. I guess I could use someone else, but I didn't want to let Fay go yet. I wanted her to stay the night and make sure she had a safe place. The thought of watching her sleep not only fascinated me, but made me feel like I'm sure Eli felt when he got that look on his face, the one he used for Clara. It pissed me off just as much as it intrigued me, just once, to know what the big deal was about.

I had to know why Eli would give up everything for it. I mean this sucked, but I could live this way if I had to. One day, I would go back to normal. I knew it. I had to.

I was a devourer. I was not a human and never would be.

I ate all the food in no time. I wasn't really into human food like Eli, but I had to put on a show for her. She actually plowed through her food, too, which surprised me because I thought human girls complained about their weight and survived on three ounces of protein a day or something. This chick ate the means of a full grown man.

"What?" she said and cocked her brow at me.

A chuckled slipped past my lips. "That's really cute."

"What?" she asked, seemingly affronted by my compliment. Another anomaly since in my experience, human girls practically begged for compliments.

I squinted. "I'm not allowed to say you're cute?"

She opened her mouth to speak, but seemed to think better of it. "I guess so. No one has said I'm cute in a long time. Sorry. Occupational hazard."

"And what occupation is that?"

"The occupation of being able to take down the guys I date," she replied smartly.

"You didn't do so well with the guy out there," I reminded her.

"He caught me off guard, number one." She pointed and drove her points home. "Number two, he confined me to a small space where I couldn't get a good swing at him. Number three, he was a lot bigger than me."

"All valid, cupcake," I goaded. This American, human girl I knew was having a hard time in her life now, but somehow I also knew at some point in her life was spoiled and pampered. A daddy's girl perhaps.

She scoffed and pushed her plate away. "Check," she called and motioned to the waitress.

I chuckled, pleased with how affected she was by me. "You're feisty for someone who was attacked not long ago." She let her gaze settle on me and shrugged before looking away. "It's a great show of character."

"Like I said, occupational hazard. I was in the military. They trained us to move on, not let things get to us."

"I don't think it was the military," I mused. "I think it was something else." Her face paled a little and I sucked in a quick breath. "There," I told her and moved toward her across the table as close as the table would allow. "Whatever that was you were just thinking about. That's what made you strong, that's what made you what you are."

She looked as if she might cry for a split second before she banished it.

"Nice one, Dr. Phil," she said easily and looked at the table. "Listen, I'm tired." She looked up at the waitress as she came and started to pull her wallet from her purse.

"No," I said gruffly and handed the waitress a fifty. "Keep the change." I stood and took Fay's arm. "Come on. You owe me."

"W-what did you do that for? The bill couldn't have been more than twenty bucks."

"Because I can and I didn't want to wait." I pulled her roughly—I knew it was too rough—out to the parking lot and searched for something, anything. "Fay, I need you to keep up your end of the bargain. Find me someone who's fighting or upset. I don't want to…"

"What?" she asked and it was the first time all night she'd been frightened of me.

"Just, please." I stepped closer slowly. "Fay, please."

"Do you have some fetish or something or are we back to vampires?" she said wryly.

My vision blurred a little and I groaned. "Whichever one makes you want to help me."

She sighed. "There's no one here." I started to speak, but she held up her hand. "I know where we can go if you promise to…" she sighed and threw her hands up in exasperation, "to not get me murdered in an alley or something."

"I'll keep you safe. I promise. I like having you around, Fay."

I jolted at the realization. I couldn't stop myself from saying the first thing that popped into my head. She seemed to recognize that I had made a mistake and smiled a little. "Okay. Okay, Enoch, I'll go on this crazy, wild goose chase of an adventure with you tonight. But tomorrow, I'm back on my own wild goose chase, all right?"

"What are you searching for?"

"My sister. I haven't seen her in a very long time, and last I heard, she moved out here with her new husband. I was…discharged from the military so I'm hoping that she'll want to see me."

I grimaced. "Family's overrated."

"That's what I used to think," she said softly, "until you don't have any left."

I sucked in a ragged breath at tasting her sorrow. Ever since that day in the alley, things didn't even taste the same. The emotions that I used to relish in now tasted like acid, and though I needed them to survive, I didn't enjoy them anymore. She looked at me curiously. "Wait, if we're looking for someone who's fighting or upset, then what about sad?"

"If they're really sad, that'll work," I answered automatically · and regretted it. "But not as well as anger does."

"I'm really sad," she insisted and started to come toward me. "Use me for your little experiment."

"No," I insisted back, but it came out a growl.

She faltered for a split second, but kept coming. "Why not?"

"Because." Whatever she was thinking about must have been awful because the sorrow was eating her alive. I groaned just as she reached me and opened my mouth to protest, but her sadness filled it instead. I looked down at her through eyes barely still open and watched as she remembered whatever it was that was making her so sad. Right before her chest shook, I moaned and licked my lip, unable to stop myself. She seemed enthralled by this and taken aback simultaneously.

"Fay, stop," I pleaded.

"It's not real," she said into the air, as if she needed to say it, to convince herself.

I took her face in my hands and that one small gesture solidified my fate. Oh, no... Was this what Eli felt when he met Clara? Some unknown reason and pull to know her? To know why she mattered and ticked all of sudden out of all the people and women in all the world? Why this one person?

Why her...to make me feel?

I let my thumb run across her cheekbone and realized in the hundreds of years that I'd lived, I'd never taken the time to just see what a woman felt like.

Anger rolled over me at the fact that my life as I knew it was over. I was a dead man, for all intents and purposes. I couldn't go home again. It wasn't her fault; I was just finally coming to terms that I had changed. And there wasn't any going back.

"Fay, please don't think about what happened to you. I don't want to...feel that. I don't want to...feed off of you. I don't like it. Let's find someone else, all right?"

She gulped, looking up at me. "You truly believe you can feed off of my emotions."

"Humor me," I said and smiled cockily to bring some of the snap back to the conversation. I swept her hair behind her ear as I let her go, stepping back. "Let's just find what we need and then I'll get you a soft, warm place to sleep."

She sighed. "All right. You're clearly insane, but all right."

She eyed me as she pulled her cell out. She asked the person on the line for a cab at the motel. We sat side-by-side on the curb in comfortable silence for ten minutes waiting for it. When we got in, she told him to take us to the shipping yards. I looked at her curiously. She sat with a little knowing smile on her lips.

Three
Fay

I stepped from the cab and looked around at my surroundings. I knew there was a bar around here somewhere. Where there was a bar, there was a bar fight not too far away. If vampire boy over here wanted to get his kicks by watching somebody get his lights punched out, then fine. As long as I didn't have to sleep on a park bench with cold fog coming from my mouth all night, I could deal with a little crazy from this guy.

I had dealt with far worse.

The guy was so weak, I had to help him from the cab. I didn't know if he just needed a good night's sleep or what. A meal hadn't helped him any.

"Are you going to be all right?" He sighed and I heard him gulp as we walked. "We probably should have just went to the hotel."

"That wouldn't have been good for you," I heard him mutter low under his breath.

I rolled my eyes. "Sticking with it, eh?" He stayed silent. "Fine. But if you pass out, I'm calling an ambulance and then I'm out."

He chuckled, his voice rough, but still managing to be amazingly sexy as it skated across my cheek.

"Okay, blue eyes." I shook with goose bumps, unable to contain them, and he groaned a little, whispering, "Bloody hell. You're killing me, little human."

"It's cold," I lied. It *was* cold, but that was absolutely not the reason for the goose flesh. He knew it and I knew it. And I hated it. I didn't like for people to get under my skin. It made me feel too vulnerable, like they had power over me. When they had power, they could hurt you, leave you, die and leave you destroyed. I wasn't up for any more of that. Except for Clara; she was already attached to me and I owed it to her.

He looked over. Even in the dark with barely any light being provided from the streetlamps, I could see his purple eyes searching mine. "Just help me and then you never have to see me again."

It was almost like he could tell what I'd been thinking about.

Before I could open my mouth to rebut, someone calling Enoch's name followed by a throaty laugh was heard from behind us. We both looked over our shoulders to find a tall redhead standing there. She was smirking in a way that showed her obvious enjoyment. "Oh, Enoch. It's delightful to see you again, babe."

"Don't *babe* me, turncoat," he growled back. He looked over at me, suddenly furious and shook me off. "And you. Get out of here and stop hanging on me like a bloody leech." I felt my eyes go wide. Excuse me? I opened my mouth and his grip tightened on my arm. "I said. Get. Out. Of. Here. You stupid little human."

I yanked my arm away and bumped his shoulder hard as I passed him. I heard his sigh as I did so. It was relief, and I knew exactly what he was doing. I turned the corner to the building and stopped at the edge where they couldn't see me.

He had been trying to get me away from the situation quickly, that was obvious, and he thought the quickest way was to upset me. It was a tactical move, but why? What was going on? I strained to listen but not make a sound. I calmed myself down, breathing slowly.

I could hear the redhead speaking, even as people came in and out of the bar across the street. "You should have stayed with the rebels, Enoch. At least there, you might have stood a chance. Now, you're just going to die alone, here, on this dock."

"You going to take me out by yourself?" Enoch asked her.

"Oh, I'm not by myself," she answered with a laugh and walked around him once slowly, stalking him like a cat as he stood still, as if he knew what was coming. "Don't you know me better than that?"

He began to take slow steps backward toward the alley. I pressed further in, making sure not to be seen. I couldn't bring myself to leave. Enoch had saved me when he could have just walked away, even when he clearly was weak or sick or in withdrawals…whatever was wrong with him. He hadn't left me; I wasn't leaving him. One thing I had learned was that no matter what, you didn't leave someone behind. Not only was it a douchey thing to do, but it would come back to bite you—eventually.

I had left Clara behind and was paying that price every day.

I strained to see but not be seen as she came back around to his front. He was perfectly still, almost inhumanly so. She pulled something from the bag draped across her chest and he hissed, taking another step back, another step closer to me. "Wow, Ang, you're really going to stick that thing in me? You're going to take the rebels' ways and use them against our kind?"

"Isn't that what you did to the Horde at Arequipa?" she seethed.

"How did you make it out alive, by the way? I thought you'd be worm food at Resting Place by now."

She gripped his throat with speed that didn't look possible. I blinked as he choked and took a step back, throwing her arm off. He stepped again, but she followed. "These legs are for more than just looking good."

He scoffed and I wondered why he was so intent on antagonizing her when she clearly had something over him. "Did you really just say that, red?"

I looked on the ground of the alley for something while they bickered. A metal pipe was all I could find, but it would do. I would help Enoch and then we'd be even-steven. The closer they got, the more heated their words were. She was practically screeching by then and I rolled my eyes at the fact that I used to be just like her. So dramatic and thought I was so entitled. You know, except for the drug dealer part, which she clearly had to be.

I peeked out again and wondered if the reason he wasn't fighting back was because she was a girl. She slammed his head with the side of her fist, but his head barely moved. "Tell me where they are."

"I haven't seen them since I left."

"You're lying."

"He's a human now," he growled and I fought to keep my breaths even. Human now? As opposed to what? "I don't want anything to do with him."

"I know that the Enoch I used to know would be telling me the truth right now, but I don't even know who you are." She gripped his neck and this time, he couldn't push her off. She squeezed and lifted him just a tad so only his toes were touching the ground. I watched and couldn't believe what my eyes were seeing. How could she be doing that? That wasn't possible. Even for a really strong person, that wasn't possible. "You're not feeding," she said steadily and my lips fell open. "You're bringing yourself to the point of starvation and probably trying to live off emotions that aren't forced, just like Eli had been doing."

Eli was Clara's husband's name, too.

"Then kill me and get it over with."

She shook her head. "Why, Enoch? What happened to make you do this? What did Eli do to you?"

"Nothing," he groaned and scratched at her arm. "Eli had nothing to do with this."

"I don't believe you. There is a reason for this. Devourers don't just turn soft. It's not in our nature to. I don't know why or how, but Eli did something to you and I'm going to find out what. He won't get away with this. He won't do this to someone else. We're going to stop those rebels once and for all." She must have squeezed tighter because he began to choke harder. "I'll avenge you, Enoch. I'm going to make him pay for what he's done to you."

I didn't think; I let my nature—my basic instincts—take over, and moved forward swiftly in the dark behind her and cracked the steel pipe over her head. Enoch fell to the ground coughing and cursing. I moved to help him, knowing he was going to be angry with me for not leaving. I didn't realize how angry, however.

"What the bloody hell are you still doing here?" he growled and jerked his arm away from my outstretched hand.

"Saving you, looks like."

"Saving me!" he scoffed and stood, coughing the last bit as he looked around. "That is rich, little girl. Now you've done it. I tried to be the good guy and you instead had to be the big bad girl who saves the day, didn't you?" His voice went up a few octaves as he mocked me. "Oh, look at me, I'm such a chick, I think it's a good idea to sleep in my car in the middle of the night in a seedy neighborhood. Oh, look at me, I'm such a girl, I agree to get rooms with complete strangers for the night because I have nowhere else to go." His voice was getting lower and more back to normal the louder and angrier he got. He moved toward me as he spoke. "And bloody hell, I think I'll stick around and get myself killed after I've already been told to get lost when I see someone about to get his block knocked off when it's obvious I have no business being there to begin with!"

I felt the wall slam into my back and my eyes went as wide as they could go. I was staring at something that wasn't possible. It was being fed to me in small pieces, this puzzle. He had said it, she had said it, and now I was staring it in the face—he wasn't human.

His neck and arms were lined in little blue veins that had only popped out when he'd gotten truly angry. All I could do was stand there and stare because I was truly, honestly, to my very core, terrified. Of him? Of what was going on? Of the fact that there was obviously things in the world that I didn't want to know about? I didn't know. But right then, I just knew that he was angry and looking at me as if he wanted to hit something. And I was the only thing that was around.

I felt the breaths as they escaped my lips, in and out, but I didn't move. His eyes searched my face for several long seconds that seemed longer than they actually were, I was sure, before he seemed to snap back onto himself. He looked down at my mouth and back to my eyes. Then his gaze wandered to his arm to find the little blue rivers, seemingly no surprise there, then back to my eyes. He sighed and took a deep breath, closing his eyes for a few beats before opening them, all the while keeping his hands at his sides, his fists tight.

"Fay," he said slowly as he looked right into my eyes, "don't be afraid of me."

"You weren't lying," I whispered, "about needing to feed. You're not human. I heard her say it and now…"

"Just don't be afraid of me," he commanded softly and stared into my eyes. Weirdly, I felt calm—almost too calm—but I knew he wasn't going to hurt me. He kept saving me. Why would he hurt me if he kept doing that? I nodded. He nodded back. "Good. Now," he scowled now that that little…impediment seemed to be out of the way. "Why didn't you leave when I told you to? I was a jackass to you. Why would you stay?"

"I knew you were just being mean to get me to leave." His scowled deepened. "And I knew you were just getting me to leave to keep me safe. You saved me earlier at the hotel when you could have just left and kept going, but you didn't. You helped me. It wasn't right to leave you, especially when you were so weak."

He groaned in a huff, looking at my throat, anywhere but my eyes in that moment. "I'm not weak, I'm—"

"I'm not hurting your ego—"

He laughed, a scoff more than anything. "Oh, really!"

"I'm just stating a fact. You were weak. Whatever is going on with you…whatever it is, you're not doing well," I finished, sucking my breaths in slowly through my trembling lips. He noticed and watched them as he spoke.

"You going to lie to me and say you're cold again, little human?" he sneered, but his eyes were soft and I could tell it was all a front. He was just like me. He pushed people away so he didn't have to deal with them. So he didn't *have* to feel. Being alone was better than being disappointed. Someone had disappointed him before and he was trying his hardest to nip this in the bud.

"No," I breathed and lifted my hand to touch his arm. He pulled back, but I didn't let him get away. I grabbed his wrist quickly and turned it over in my hands. I could hear his breath hissing through his teeth at my forehead as I looked down at our hands. "I'm not cold. I'm afraid."

"I told you not to be afraid," he said softly. He pushed my fingers away gently and held my hand captive to stop my searching. "You won't find any blue veins. It only happens when we can't…contain our anger." I looked up to find him watching me closely, curiously.

"What are you?" I dared to ask though I knew…

"No, Fay."

"Why?"

"I need to get you out of here," he said, but didn't move. "You need to get as far away from me as possible. Run and don't look back. Don't ever think of me again."

I sighed and screwed up my lips. "That's not going to happen. How can I forget?" He took a deep breath and it gave me pause as his grip on my hand tightened just a bit, just enough to be telling. "Can you...make me forget?"

"No," he answered quickly. "I can only help you feel better about things with my persuasion. Help you feel comfortable with a decision."

"I don't want to leave," I said harder. "I need to find my sister. She's close. Don't you dare send me away."

"That's good." He nodded, his black hair ruffling in the cold wind. "As long as you're not with me." I winced at his words a little, unable to stop myself. He saw and smiled a little, the cruel face making a reappearance. "Don't forget that I don't want you here. You need to leave as soon as possible." He looked around and then down at the redhead. He jerked his gaze back up to mine. "In fact, I'll get you a cab right now."

"Why are you so afraid? What happened to you?"

He didn't pretend to not understand. "I'm not afraid, Fay. I'm just not a good person. You don't want to know me. Trust me on this. I'm doing you a favor."

He pulled me forward by my arm out to where the alley met the street. "I don't believe you." I tripped over the stony road and he yanked me back up. "I don't believe you!" I said louder. "You're being a coward."

"Why do you want to stay with me?" he asked harshly, turning me to face him. "You know that I'm not human. I'm. Not. Human." He stared for effect. It was working. I gulped. "Why do you want to stay with me?"

I decide for once in my miserable life since my parents died, I'd tell the whole truth, nothing but the truth, so help me, God. "Because I try to be tough, but I'm not always. Because I might get into trouble again and there won't be another good guy there to save me like you did. Because being alone sucks," he sucked in a hard breath, but I kept going, "and I'm so close, I know it. I just want to find my sister and I'm afraid that I won't and I'll be alone forever."

He shook his head, his breathing rushing in and out. He squeezed his eyes shut. "Stop. I don't want to feed off your sorrow." He opened his eyes slowly, almost as if testing me to see if I'd still be there. He glanced back where we'd been and cursed. "I've got to get you out of here."

"What—" I looked back to see the redhead groaning and getting up. She was awake and rolling up to her feet. Impossible! "She needs stitches at the very least!" I protested. "She—"

"She isn't human," he explained. I sighed and ran as he pulled me behind him. "She'll be fully aware in a minute and be fully pissed on top of that. We need to—"

A loud bang rang out through the alley as it ricocheted off the buildings. I covered my ears and looked behind me, expecting the redhead to be coming up the rear, but there was no one. When I turned back to face Enoch, his hand was outstretched in a fist in front of his face. When he opened his fist, a bullet fell to the road with a dull clang and my lungs refused to cooperate. "You caught that?" I whispered my anguished question. "Enoch?"

He pushed me behind him roughly and kept his arm around me from behind. To keep me calm, to keep me from bolting, to keep me feeling safe as he growled his words to the group of the men that had suddenly come from out of the shadows? I didn't know. But I gripped his arm tightly in response and tried with everything in me to keep it together as I looked to my left and right for a way out or something to use as a weapon.

"So who is it now?" Enoch asked in a growl and pushed me with his back, forcing me to retreat backward. "Hatch and Reece are toast. I know that for a fact. I saw it with my own eyes. So who's the piper now?"

"Maybe I am," the redhead sputtered and slithered her hand up one of the men's arm. He shook her arm off and glowered at her.

"You can't even get a simple task done correctly, Angelina. He should be dead now instead of pestering us, but instead I'm going to have to kill him to get to the girl." I gasped and felt Enoch's hand tighten painfully on my arm.

"The girl is a human," he growled. "I picked her up a motel and was about to have my way with her before Angelina butted in." His breaths puffed in the air in front of him. "What could you possibly want with a stupid feeler?"

I flinched at the insult—not clearly understanding it—though I knew he was just trying to save me. The man tilted his head, clearly not fazed by Enoch's speech. "She's going to lead us to Clara."

I gasped, unable to stop it. "Clara! What do you want with Clara?"

They all stood silent except for the man who had been speaking. He smiled. It was the most evil thing I'd ever seen. I covered my mouth with my palm, knowing my mistake had been grave, knowing I'd given the enemy exactly the ammo they'd wanted. I didn't know why they wanted Clara. That didn't make any sense. But it was Enoch's reaction that surprised me the most. He looked at me over his shoulder, his jaw clenched, his eyes angry. "How the hell do you know Clara?"

I felt my lips part. I dug my nails into his arm. "How the hell do you?" I whispered.

"That's enough of the family tree for now," the man said with a chuckle. "Just send her on over and we'll be on our way."

"What for?" Enoch growled, still looking at my face.

"Bait." I heard the smile in his voice. "Come on. Red rover, red rover, send Fay right over."

Enoch sighed and pushed me back even further as he turned to face them again.

"Do you trust me?" he asked in a low voice as he pushed harder and faster.

"Yes," I answered without hesitation.

His eyes closed at that admission. "Hold on tight to me."

In a second before I could think of what he was doing, he snatched me against his chest and sent us sailing over the dock's edge into the water. I could hear cursing and yelling, even some loud bangs that had to be gunshots, but I just held on tight.

A deep voice boomed, "Don't shoot! We need her alive!"

We landed in the freezing water and he pulled me under further and further. We swam hard toward the opposite dock. If we surfaced before we made the cover of it, they'd kill us for sure.

The deeper and further we got, the more I tried to stay calm and hold my breath, feeling the burn and ache in my lungs. I needed to take a breath soon. I was trained in holding my breath. I had been put in a chamber with tear gas when I went through boot camp, more than once. I knew how to hold my breath. But we'd been under for a long time.

I started to panic and began to fight him. He didn't understand that I couldn't *not* breathe like him, that I need air more often—and then his lips were on mine. I couldn't see much in the murky water, but I could see that his eyes were open. I tensed, still fighting inside, but he held tight and smoothed my cheek with his thumb. I relaxed my muscles, and opened my mouth under his, blowing my air from my nose. He wasted no time in giving me new air in return.

I worried about him for a split second before I remembered that he wasn't human, number one, and number two, if he was offering obviously he had some to spare. He leaned back and nodded his head as if to ask if I was good to go. I nodded back and he pulled me forward, putting a hand under my butt and pushing me forward to give me a boost. He stayed right behind the whole way. As soon as I saw the docks in the water, it was like a cue for my body to gain some little spurt of energy. Adrenaline.

I took off, determined to get there as fast as I could. My lungs ached and burned, and when I surfaced, I tried not to gasp and moan so loudly in case anyone was close. He surfaced in front of me and wasn't even winded. I tried to calm my breathing, but it was hard to do with him watching me so intently. "Stop it."

"What?" he asked, but the smirk he tacked on let me know that he knew exactly what was up.

"It sucks that you don't have to breathe."

"Or eat. Or sleep." Then he looked at me seriously, right into my very soul. "But you don't have to feed off anyone's emotions either. Their anger, their hatred, to taste it on your tongue."

I shivered and wrapped my arms around myself. "I'm sorry."

"Why are you sorry?"

"For thinking about my sister even after you asked me not to." My teeth chattered. "I don't know what sorrow tastes like, but I can imagine it's not good."

He sighed and ran a hand through his hair, sidelining my subject. "We can go. You have to get out of this water."

"I'm fine," I lied. "We should wait and make sure it's safe."

"You're freezing to death," he barked back. "I'll handle them. It should take them a long time to make it to this side of the docks. Let's go and get you that room I promised you. And you can tell me how you know Clara Hopkins."

I shivered again as he said my sister's name, because the amount of malice that came with it made my skin crawl.

Four
Enoch

It wasn't the first time I'd hotwired a car and it wouldn't be the last. Miss goody two-shoes hadn't protested, which meant she either really wanted to see her sister or she was a lot colder than she was letting on. Her lips had begun to take on a slight bluish tint. I debated going to the hospital instead of the hotel, but she assured she was fine. Her logic was if we stole a nice car, chances are that the person would have good insurance and wouldn't be hurt financially from it. If we stole a beater or some hunk of junk like I had planned to do, then some poor sap would more than likely be losing his only means of transportation and have no way to replace said transportation. She had a point, I guess. So I cranked the heat as high and as hot as it would go as soon as we got into the black as night Lexus IS C.

The GPS in the car told the opposite direction of the docks was west. Perfect. I followed the roads out, trying to block the sounds of human chattering teeth, and fled as quickly as I could without drawing attention to ourselves. It would have taken them twenty minutes to drive the distance to the opposite dock and it was getting close to fifteen. I wanted to be long gone before they were close.

Clara and Eli must be in the midst of a big rebel camp for them to be searching so diligently for them. I looked over at her blue tinted lips and knew that even though she was going to be fine, she was still uncomfortably cold. Her teeth still chattered against each other and it pissed me off how much I hated that sound. I shouldn't care, but I did. I looked around the car and actually made a noise in the back of my throat at what I found. I pulled the jacket from the back and placed it around her as quickly as I could and still drive carefully.

She looked at me in surprise. "Thanks."

"You're teeth are still chattering," I barked.

"It doesn't work like that. It's bone-deep," she muttered. "I need a hot bath, then I'll be fine."

I stayed quiet, letting her fall asleep, and drove the next three hours in complete silence. She slept restlessly and I knew she wasn't really resting, but her body was forcing her to sleep. She turned and tossed, pulling the jacket up to her neck over and over. I pulled into a motel and left her in the car to get a room. A motel was less conspicuous. People usually rented motels by the week, not the night. And it was all ground level—easier to keep watch.

I parked in the back by the fence and trash bins. I snuck out quietly and came out with the old brass hotel key in my hand. I stopped when I saw the door to the car open. I blinked and turned in a circle in the dark parking lot.

"Fay?" I hissed and ran to the car as quickly as I could, not even caring if someone saw the blur of it. The jacket was on the seat, but she was gone. I turned and searched the lot with my eyes, but couldn't move from that spot. Why would she leave the car? Or did someone take her? Had they caught up to us so quickly and I hadn't noticed? Had I let them take her because I'd been so preoccupied? "Fay!" I yelled.

My shoulders slouched. I should've been happy, but I was anything but. She wasn't mine to keep. I was on a mission to find my brother and she had just been a distraction anyway. I shook my head '*no*'. That was until I found out she knew Clara.

I scrubbed my face with my fist and cursed as I slammed her door. When I turned back to the hotel, I saw a swath of dark hair as it rounded the corner. I felt my brows come together. Once again, not caring who saw me, I blurred over to the building and didn't stop until I was right behind whoever the woman was. I grabbed her arm and made her turn to face me.

She gasped and pushed hard into my chest—this intruder's chest—with the palm of her hand. The tears on her cheek and chin cracked something inside of me. Her eyes met mine and her lips opened to release a strangled noise that sounded like a plea more than anything else.

"You left me," she accused.

"I went to get a room."

She sighed and let her hand fall from my chest. I kept her arm in my hand however. "You parked in the back of the lot in the dark. I was alone when I woke up." She sniffed. There it was again. The cracking in my chest. "I thought…you left me."

"Why would I do that?" I growled, so completely pissed with how she controlled me. She didn't know it, but she did. I was actually scared in that parking lot back there. Scared! Me! Scared that something had happened to her. And here she sat crying beside the motel because she thought I left her. Why did she care anyway?

Ahh…. I nodded. "Ah. Thought you were going to have to sleep outside again, huh?" She squinted, but I grinned. "Don't worry, princess." I shook the room key in front of her face. "I got you that room, just like I promised."

I didn't let go of her arm as I practically dragged her to the other side of the motel. I unlocked the door and pulled her inside. She didn't say a word, just crawled into the bed.

"I thought you were going to take a hot bath?"

She sniffed again and pulled the covers up to her chin. "I just want to sleep."

I locked the door and turned to look at her, tightening my fists. She was facing away from me. "I thought you said you needed a hot bath to feel better, so you wouldn't be cold anymore. I can't think with your teeth chattering—"

She sighed so quietly, but it still stopped me dead. "Enoch…just leave me alone, okay?"

And then her sadness hit me. I gripped the arm of the chair as I eased into it and tried not to make an audible sound that would let her know I was feeding from her. Her grief threatened

to swallow me where I sat. I didn't dare move as I bore through
my body's acceptance of what she was offering. She didn't even
know what she was doing. Her shoulders shook a little under the
covers. I knew she was crying still, but she had no idea that by
doing so she was sending that putrid taste right to me.

I gripped the fabric so hard in my fists that I heard it tear
under my fingers. I opened my eyes to find she had rolled over
and was staring at me in astonishment. Her eyes were even wetter
than they'd been outside.

I felt so guilty knowing that I was the reason that she'd been
crying outside and I may even be the reason she was crying now.

Guilt. *Me.*

I knew I was being an ass—I was doing it on purpose. I didn't
want her to like me, not even a sliver, but it still hurt to think
that I was causing this human more pain when she was obviously
in so much already.

"What does sadness taste like?" she whispered. "Or sorrow,
grief, or...loss?"

I let my death grip on the poor cheap polyester go and
leaned my head back, closing my eyes so I didn't have to look at
her when I answered.

"Rotten." She gasped, but I kept my eyes closed. "It didn't
always taste that way. Back in the day, I reveled in the taste. It was
what you could imagine your favorite drug would feel like. Sweet
and heady, heavy, but light and creamy. I chased it and produced
it. I would have done anything for it. I lived off it. It's what
devourers do. We survive off emotion and I never wanted
anything else." I peeked my eyes open, unable to stop myself. I
needed to see the look of hate she had to be sending me so I

could get her out of my mind and think of this as the mission it was, move on, and stop looking at this human as some…prize. Some…girl.

My eyes met hers and she was studying me. It was clear she was waiting for more of the story, giving me the benefit of the doubt. There wasn't a trace of hate, judgment, or disgust in her eyes as she watched me. She just waited, knowing with certainty, that there was more to tell.

I had never had someone have faith in me before.

I gritted my teeth. "What?" I barked. "You don't believe that I'm the monster I say I am? You think that just because you've only seen the tame me that I'm not—"

"I believe you," she interrupted and shook her head. She sighed and shivered, pulling the blanket around herself tighter. "What I don't understand is why you're trying so hard to make me hate you."

I snorted. "So you don't get any girly notions that this trip is anything but what it is." I crossed my ankle over my leg and glared at her to drive my point home. "Now—how do you know Clara?"

She scoffed, barely. She gave me a sad look and then rolled back over. "Goodnight, Enoch."

I wanted to fight with her, but knew when her breathing was slow and steady not even two minutes later that I had made the right decision in letting her sleep. She was exhausted.

I grumbled under my breath and rolled my eyes. I didn't know how to take care of a human. They needed to sleep and eat and all sorts of things that I took for granted. I loved to sleep. It was one of my favorite pastimes, but I didn't need to do it.

Human bodies were useless. They gave out on them daily. Every day they had to recharge. What was that about? That sucked. Eating three times a day. Going to the bathroom constantly. And now here I was, dragging this human across the United States and she was pissed at me, which was what I had wanted, and I still needed to feed. The fight with the Horde earlier had helped a lot, but her little sorrow session had barely tipped the iceberg of what I needed to survive.

Tomorrow, I was going to be right back where I started, dragging, needing to feed, and cranky as all get out.

I scrubbed my face with my hands and looked over her. I got up and walked over to look down at her, checking her forehead to make sure her skin was warm and normal temperature. She felt normal enough temperature wise, but her skin… I moved my fingers to her cheek, remembering when I had touched her cheek in the water to reassure her. She had been about to freak and it was all I could think to do.

She was softer than any woman had a reason to be. I thought back to that night in the alley. She was softer than that woman, too. I closed my eyes against the onslaught of memories. Maybe I was going about this all wrong. Maybe being an ass to this woman wasn't the best way. She'd been through a lot and she had tried to help me. And just now when I explained what I was and how I lived…how I fed…there was no judgment in her eyes. No fear.

I smoothed her hair behind her ear and pulled the covers up to her chin. Then I pulled the blanket off the other bed and placed it on top of her, too. She moaned and squirmed around to get cozy, sighing happily as if the warmth helped things. I felt that sigh all the way to my gut, though I would never admit it to anyone.

I settled back into the chair and found myself staring at her face all night until morning. She opened her eyes when the light through the curtains made its way across the room, reaching her and saying its hello. I decided to spend this new day in a different way. I was Enoch, the ass everybody hated and thought was a bastard, but who I chose to be now that I had a fresh start, a clean slate? That was just that—my choice. She didn't know me from Adam. For whatever reason, I was given a clean slate in that alley that night. I was a different devourer now and it was my choice what I did from now on.

She looked at me and then at the bedspread. She studied those ugly, tacky fabric triangles. "Did you sit there all night?" she asked softly.

I smiled slightly. "Why don't you go get your hot bath now. Then I'll buy you some breakfast before we hit the road."

five
fay

I took my time drying my hair, wanting it not to just be dry, but be straight. Enoch seemed different today, less angry at me for existing, and I wasn't ready to face him. He was going to ask questions about Clara and I didn't know if I wanted to tell him or not.

I used the blow dryer to air out the shirt I had been wearing a little. It was pointless, but it made me feel better on some unconscious level. Really, I was just stalling.

I sighed loudly and got dressed, stalling no more. Cracking open the bathroom door, I didn't see him in the room. I fully opened the door so fast and so hard that it banged on the wall, leaving a hole in the cheap sheetrock. The hotel door was yanked open then and Enoch stormed in. "What? What happened?"

"Where did you go?"

He squinted. "I was checking the motel's perimeter before we left. Making sure we hadn't been followed." He said the last part slowly and looked at my throat and then my chest. He was taking note of my breathing, I realized, which was erratic. I tried to calm down. "Where did you think I had gone?"

"Nowhere." I moved to put my shoes on, but he grabbed my arm by the elbow and stopped me. "Will you stop manhandling me like some—"

"Where did you think I went?" he asked again, so close his breath swept across my eyelashes. His eyes were lidded, grimacing, like he was working something out in his mind.

"Let me go. Don't worry about it. You're here. It doesn't matter."

"Answer me," he bit out.

I huffed. "I thought you left, okay! Everybody leaves," I breathed the words vehemently and hated being so open and vulnerable to him of all people. He didn't care about me. Yes, he saved me. Why? I didn't know, but it wasn't because he cared. There was a reason and he was going to tell me soon enough. He was a calculating person. He didn't do things without having a plan and purpose.

He didn't let go; in fact, I could have sworn he moved a half an inch closer. "You thought I left for good. You thought I abandoned you last night, too." I looked away, down at his neck, but the cords of skin and muscle did nothing to help with calming my breathing. "Why would I save you, twice, just to abandon you in some random spot on the trip? I think it's obvious that there's something more going on here, and you know it."

I sucked in a small, quick breath and looked up at him. He was so close I couldn't breathe.

"Clara?" I sneered and wanted to laugh at how jealous it sounded.

He swallowed and I saw the clouds roll in behind his eyes.

"Clara has nothing to do with the fact that you know what I am. I didn't know you knew Clara when I saved you the first time. Now did I?" I pressed my lips together, but couldn't look away from those violet eyes. I shuddered and shook with goose bumps, causing his eyes to travel down my neck and shoulders. He sighed. "You're killing me, little human," he whispered.

I stared up at him, stunned that he was being so bold with me. He usually acted as though being in the same room with me was a chore in itself and now he was actually letting me see him. He was affected by…me? I didn't see how that was possible when he was this beefy, worldly, not-human devourer and I was a very human and sometimes neurotic girl whose sadness he could literally taste. How was there anything appealing about that?

I shook my head and steeled my back. "How do you know my sister?"

He seemed surprised and released my arm gently. "Sister," he repeated and crossed his arms. "Put your shoes on." I glared up at him sullenly and he tacked on a, "Please."

As soon as we were sitting down at the cheap diner, he began to ask his questions, which didn't surprise me in the least.

"So you're the sister that joined the military and left Clara to live with the pastor and his family."

That wasn't really a question, but he was definitely implying some things he wanted me to answer. I sighed and swallowed down the guilt, hoping he couldn't already taste it this early in the conversation. I scoffed and shook my head. Wow, I was so calm about all this devourer business. I looked up at him and saw him watching me closely.

"Yes. I'm the sister that freaked when our parents died and abandoned her little sister to live with the pastor so I didn't have to deal with her. She was our parents' favorite and I didn't want to have to console her when I didn't even know how to console myself. We had nothing. No money, no house, no car. Everything was gone. All I got was a lousy thirteen hundred bucks from the stuff that sold after all the bills were paid. Clara and I both were a little spoiled by our father. He tried to pretend that we had more money than we did. He was a good man, but we had no idea how to take care of ourselves. So I took that little bit of money, all I had left in the world, and I ran like the coward I was and didn't look back."

I felt a tear race down my cheek as I stared at the tabletop. So much for not letting him taste my sadness so early on, huh?

"What can I get you...folks?" I glanced up at the waitress to see her sympathetic gaze and wiped my cheek. "Oh, honey. It's not as bad as all that, is it?" She sent Enoch a small glare and a nod. "Is it this one?" Enoch was still looking at me and hadn't spared her a glance. "I'll toss him out on his keister if you say the word."

I shot my gaze over to Enoch at that, who was chuckling silently.

"That won't be necessary." I looked back up at her. She was tall and thin, middle-aged and so normal looking. She was someone's mother for sure. "But thank you. I'll just take a coffee and whatever's on special."

"Okay, sugar."

"She'll have pancakes, a side of bacon, and bring us some fruit, too, please," Enoch interrupted, his voice as smooth and creamy as the coffee I was craving. "I'll take the same exact thing, just double it." He winked at her. "And thanks for looking out for her. She's having a rough time right now. It's hard for her to let people look out for her so I appreciate the help." He reached over and rubbed his thumb over my chin to collect the last tear. I gasped so quietly, it didn't sound like a gasp at all but more like an inhale. He smirked at my shocked expression. "What? I remembered your pancakes and bacon."

"I can see that." I wiped my fingers across where his fingers had just swiped. Was he purposely trying to toy with me?

The waitress looked more stunned than I did. "Uh...I'll just put this order in then."

"Thanks, Patricia," he said, still looking at me.

"How did you—"

"Nametag." He turned with a smile and nodded his head toward it. "You're wearing a nametag, Patricia."

"Oh, right." She took her beet red cheeks and sprinted to the back to put our order in.

"You did that on purpose," I said, but smiled a little. "You know you have this effect on people and you do it on purpose to see if you can get a rise out of them."

His smile was crooked, like he knew it, but there was more to it. "You see, that's the way it used to be. But then this girl named Fay came along." I grinned down at the table, unable to stop it, even though his antics were clear. "And she was good at not falling for my charms."

I met his eyes and went for it, decided to let the old Fay come to the surface—the Fay who wasn't afraid of anyone or anything, the Fay who got what she wanted. "You used your charms on me?"

He leaned back in his seat and smiled the smile of a caught man. "You know what I mean."

"Not really. You've been barking orders and acting like I ran over your dog since I met you."

He licked his lip and actually looked a little guilty. I didn't think that was possible. I felt my eyebrows rise as he said, "When you've lived as long as I have and been brought up a certain way to believe certain things, it's going to take more than one night and a beautiful girl with a golden soul to make you change. But I am trying," he grated out, his words sounding as if they were being dragged over concrete.

But the only thing I heard was… "Beautiful?" I barely whispered. Why had I said that? "I'm…sorry." I looked up from the table to find his mouth slightly open as he watched me, his violet eyes half open. I slid out and stood.

"Where are you going?"

I scoffed with a smile. "Anywhere but here?" He smiled and huffed a laugh. I sighed. "The bathroom. I'm going to the bathroom."

"Okay, Fay." As I passed him I heard, "Don't stay gone on my account."

I groaned and wondered why I was so weird all of a sudden. I used to be a dating guru. My friends all came to me for advice because I was good at it. I had dates every weekend in high school. It was never an issue for me. And now, there I sat, babbling about...*am I beautiful?* I scoffed. Who cares if he thought I was beautiful or not. It was obvious he disliked me a great deal. Or woman in general. Or maybe just dating in general. Whatever.

And Clara. What if it was Clara? What if she had broken his heart?

I sighed and rolled my eyes as I washed my hands. Enough. I was going to go out there and get this over with.

I looked at myself in the mirror. I was pale and had no make-up. I pinched my cheeks a little to give them some color. I scoffed. Beautiful? That was lifetimes ago.

I sat back down and was sad to see the food still wasn't there. I got right to it, staring at the table.

"Clara is my little sister. She's three years younger than me. I joined the military and she stayed with Pastor and his wife. I don't really know much about what has happened to her since I left. We haven't...talked much. I know she got married." I can't help but choke up a bit at that. That I missed my sister's wedding and will never get to go back and do that again. In truth, I didn't even know about the wedding until it was too late. I had moved from the base and neither Clara nor the Pastor knew it. The invitation took too long to reach me and by the time it did... But that's on me. If I had just kept in touch, they would have known how to reach me. I keep going because I'll cry if I don't. "I don't even know what this Eli guy looks like or how old he is or if he's good to her."

It's quiet so long so I look up. He's watching me again. Just watching. His lips smile, just barely. "Eli is a good looking guy. I can tell you that much." I squint, confused, but before I can ask he continues. "And he's good to her, by human standards I'm sure. By devourer standards, it makes me want to puke. As for how old he is, I don't think that really matters. Love is love, right?"

"I can't imagine her in love. Not really. She was so…shallow and all over this stupid meathead from school. For this turnaround, so quickly…it scares me. It makes no sense for Clara to act this way. This isn't my sister at all. Which leads me to wonder…what the hell did this Eli guy do to her?" I ask softly.

His lip curls a little. "He fell in love." He looked me in the eye. "And he took her down with him. It's true. Honest to God. I saw it for myself. All the barf-inducing, sugary sweet crap. It was all real."

"Why did they have to move into the freaking woods in the middle of nowhere? What has she gotten herself into?" I whisper to myself, but look up at him. "Does this have something to do with your kind?"

"Not just my kind."

"There's more?" I whisper in a small shriek. He leans on the table, sighing and closing his eyes for a second longer than normal. "Fay," he groaned. "Please." He opened his eyes. "I'm not going to let anything happen to you. I'm going to get you to your sister. That's a promise."

"Why?" I leaned on the table, too, and into his space. "Why are you helping me? It's obvious you don't like me. Is it Clara? You and Clara had a thing and you're going to break them up or something?"

He scoffed so loud and glared. "No," he boomed. "Absolutely not. Clara Hopkins ruined my life."

I sat back in surprise. "Um..."

"She is the reason that I can't feed the way I need to," he bit out. "She is the reason my brother was taken from me. She is the reason the Horde is chasing us all." He shook his head. "No, no. I'm closer to hating Clara than loving her." I sighed and swallowed. "Sorry," he said and shrugged, "but you asked.

"I don't think I did," I muttered and blinked at the waitress as she brought our food.

"Maybe not," he conceded, "but you don't have to worry about Clara. You don't need to be jealous because there is absolutely no love there." I gave him droll look. "And I won't hurt her either, because...she married my brother."

I gasped, sucking coffee into my wind pipe. While I coughed, he came and sat beside me. Rubbing a small, forceful circle in the middle of my back, he patted and turned my face to look at him. When he saw that I was okay, he asked, "Do you need mouth to mouth?" He grinned, tilting his head a little. "I'd be very obliging."

I coughed and shoved at his stomach. "All right, Casanova. Let's take it down a notch."

He lifted his hands as he returned to his side of the booth. "Hey. Just trying to save a life."

"You already did. I don't think I thanked you for that, by the way." I made sure to look at him and not be a coward.

He smiled and looked like he was about to make a joke, but then he thought better of it. "You're welcome, Fay. And it appears it was fate that brought us together." I lifted an eyebrow. "Brother and sister-in-law."

"Oh, right. That's not a coincidence. Can't be."

"No," he agreed. "It's not. We're going to find out soon enough what's going on. I'll get you there. I'll get you to Clara. I promise."

"Thank you."

He nodded his head and took a big bite of pancakes.

"So…Eli is your brother?"

He grinned. "Don't worry. I'm the better looking brother."

I laughed and rolled my eyes, dipping my bacon into my syrup and hearing him groan about how disgusting it was. He told me some things about Eli and Clara. He had been at their wedding, which broke my heart into little pieces right then and there. But again, it was no one's fault but mine. He talked about anything he thought I would want to know that happened in the very short weeks that he had known Clara.

I ate and I listened.

We drove—he drove—until the afternoon when I noticed him starting to twitch around in the seat, obliviously uncomfortable. He rubbed his thigh with the side of his fist over and over so hard I thought the fabric of his jeans was going to rip.

Then he started to tap a rhythm on the steering wheel and turned the music up louder. As Aerosmith blared over the speakers, I knew exactly what was happening. I still didn't understand why I was calm and understanding about this, but knew what I needed to do.

I thought about the night my parents died. Clara called me. I wasn't home. She was in hysterics. She had come home and found them...

Enoch's hand swung over and gripped my thigh tightly. "Stop it," he growled.

I continued to look out the window, noticing how his hand hadn't moved from my leg. I sighed. It had been so long since someone had touched me. "You need it, don't you? I can tell. You're getting all twitchy."

"And I told you that I don't want that from you," he said harshly.

I looked over. "You just want it from someone else?"

He watched the road. "Yes."

Coward.

"I'm not a coward," he said with an angry chuckle and took his hand away. My skin was cold where his hand had been. "I'm the *only one* being smart right now."

I covered my lips with two fingers. I said that out loud.

He drove for a few more minutes and then pulled off an exit. When he pulled into a bar parking lot, I got anxious. I looked over to see him still brooding, his brows drawn together. He put the car in park and looked over at me for the first time. "Stay here. Don't come in and don't get out of this car for any reason.

Lock the doors." I started to argue, but his menacing look stopped everything. "Don't."

I leaned back in my seat slowly and looked at my lap. There were two things he was going in there for and neither of them was good. He got out and stopped by his door, his hand on the top of the car. "I'll be back in a few minutes. Stay in the car, no matter what. I'm…*not* leaving you."

Then he slammed the door and sprinted inside. I watched him go, wondering what had just happened. One minute he was an absolute jerk, the next he was reassuring me he wasn't leaving me like I had thought he was last time. I wanted to take a nap, feeling tired and drawn out, but the sun was too bright, so I climbed in the back seat and turned my face toward the back. I looked at my watch. It was fifteen after three. When someone knocked, waking me, I looked at my watch and it was almost four. I looked up at his face, the sun haloing behind his head and could already tell he was better. I unlocked his door and he climbed in.

"We need to ditch this car soon and grab another. It's not smart to keep it. The cops will be looking for it." He backed out and started to drive like everything was normal. Like he hadn't just been in there feeding off someone who was sad about their wife leaving them, or fighting because of cheating on a game or pool, or the more likely option, someone who he'd been doing intimate things with that I didn't want to think about. I rolled back over and pretended that he hadn't even come back. "Hey, what's wrong with you?" he asked. Like he had no idea. Maybe he didn't.

"Nothing."

He sighed and drove faster. "I don't like doing it any more than you like knowing I do it. Soon we'll be there and you never have to see me again." I scoffed under my breath. He was such a guy for actually not really being one. "Now what?" he growled.

"Nothing," I answered again.

"I really hate that answer."

"I'm so glad you're in a better mood," I spouted sarcastically and covered my head with my arm. I slept. I dreamt of floating, rafting with Clara and our parents down the Ichetucknee River in Florida, something we did every couple of years. Then my dream moved to other dreams. I was falling, but so warm. I wrapped myself around the warmth, not understanding why it moved and even seemed to chuckle. Then I was cold all of a sudden before we were moving again. My head ached.

I moaned when I was blasted with heat, but couldn't stay asleep any longer. I woke to find myself not in a sleek black car, but an old blue Mustang with white leather. White, cold, freezing leather. I wrapped my arms around myself and sat up in the seat before climbing up in the front.

"Afternoon, sunshine," he drawled, but he seemed extra chipper about something.

I grimaced. "You're giving me whiplash, Enoch. Pick a side, already. Either you love me or you hate me. Or…" I rolled my eyes, feeling my cheeks bloom with red, "you know what I mean."

He grinned wider. "Oh, yes. I know what you mean. Do you like the new ride?"

"I never was a 'stang girl."

He laughed. Hard. Too hard. I laughed, too, because Enoch letting loose was too good to pass up joining in. "A 'stang girl, huh? Wow. We wouldn't want that." He grinned over at me. "That sounds painful."

I pushed his arm. "Shut up."

We stopped for supper not too long after that. I had about had it with crappy diner food, but that was the way it was on the road. It was getting darker. We were getting closer, and though he didn't need to sleep, per se, he said he liked to rest and wanted to get a room for the night. I didn't know if he was just doing that for me or not, but that would be an awfully nice gesture and I didn't want to give him that much credit.

We checked into the motel first and then went into the adjoining restaurant. The diner was pretty rowdy that night. There was some kind of karaoke tournament going on and we just happened to catch it on the right night. I don't think Enoch's aggravated eyebrow came down the entire time we waited for our burgers.

I laughed at him under my hand, but he somehow heard it over the loud singing and laughing.

"Oh, this is funny? If I wanted to be tortured, I could think of a hundred less painful ways," he said and sucked down the last of his drink. He waved to the waitress and she refilled his Coke and my diet.

"I pegged you for a hard liquor man."

"Booze don't do me any good, love." He smiled and leaned back in the booth, linking his hands behind his head. "I'm not built like you, remember?"

"Right," I drawled and tried not to look at his arms stretched in that shirt, but failed. I looked away as quickly as I could, but it wasn't quick enough. I saw him tick his head to the side, whether in question or trying to catch my eye. Either way, I wasn't falling for it.

I looked around the room and thought it funny that Enoch and I were the only ones not drunk and falling all over the place. Everyone else had plates of nachos and dart board games going as they listened to horrible singing and waited their turn. It was more like a bar than a diner, really. The sign was deceiving. I heard the song change—a woman singing a very sloppy rendition of *Endless Love*. I grimaced and shook my head as people got up and started dancing to it just as I saw an eager face coming my way. I turned back to Enoch and tried to act like I was engaged with him. "Oh, no," I muttered.

"What?" Enoch said and twirled the knife in his fingers. Great, he was already armed.

"Nothing. Just pretend like we're talking."

"We are talking, princess." He grinned. I think he enjoyed any opportunity to call me that.

"Talk more, smart-alec." I laughed a little louder. He looked to the side, seeing the guy almost to our table, and he shook his head at me.

"What's the matter, princess? Don't want to dance with two-left-feet-McGee?"

"No. I don't."

"Why not?"

I looked at him, meeting him stare for stare. "Fine."

"Hey, there," I heard to my right. I turned and gave him a small smile. "Would you like to dance to the cheesiest song known to man?"

I laughed. "Uh…Yeah. Sure."

I slid out, but before I could take two-left-feet-McGee's hand, a warm, familiar hand took it instead. "Sorry, buddy. This cheesy song is spoken for," Enoch's gruff voice said near my ear.

He lifted his hands in good-natured back down and walked back to his seat.

I thought Enoch was just going to sit back down and say I owed him or something, but he towed me to the dance floor, pulling me under his arm before yanking me to his chest, forcing the air right out of my lungs. I gasped a little when our chests connected, our faces so close. "You're pretty good at that."

"Over three hundred years of living will make you good at anything," he said, almost bitterly, but he smiled a little.

"Three hundred years…" I mused, but said nothing more.

"You're welcome, by the way. I promise I won't step on your cute little feet." He twirled me out and back in before dipping me back just a little and lifting me back up. I fought for breath for more than one reason.

"I can't make the same promise, sadly."

"All you need is a good leader," he said low against my temple. "Males have changed so much over the decades. When I was born, men led the dances and woman didn't have to worry about being stepped on. It was a show of pride and honor to know how to lead a lady on the dance floor."

He moved with more open moves, more swift. He pressed a hand to my back and began leading me through a dance I'd never done before or seen, but it was fun and beautiful. He had his eyes closed, and I couldn't take my eyes off him as he led me through the moves with surety and security. A few of the other couples watched with impressed smiles on their faces at Enoch's skill.

His face was so open and smooth as he focused; he looked relaxed and young. He was the most handsome he'd ever been. He was so close in that moment, I could have stolen a kiss and he couldn't have stopped me. His dark hair brushed my hand on his neck every time he turned. It sent chills down my entire being. Not goose bumps. No—these were something else entirely. He was so honest. He may be mean at times, but you couldn't say the guy wasn't honest. And he was real and could be so…caring sometimes, seemingly out of nowhere.

All I could do was hang on and try not to kiss him.

He sucked in a breath, his eyes still closed, and slowly licked his bottom lip. He let his eyes open slowly, and the song ended just as another song began. We stood there in the middle of the crowd not moving, not dancing, and me barely breathing.

His hooded eyes watched me and he seemed so surprised. His eyes searched my face as the faster dancers moved around us. I should have been embarrassed, knowing that he was tasting my want for him, but I just couldn't be. Was he really that surprised?

Someone tapped my shoulder. I expected the same guy, but I turned my face to find a new guy there. "My turn." He grinned.

"Beat it," Enoch growled.

"Hey, pal. Share the wealth, man."

I squinted. Really? I had no idea what that term meant, but it was a pretty dumb thing to say. I opened my mouth to diffuse the situation when the waitress passed by us. "Food's ready, hun!"

Enoch grabbed my hand and pushed me in front of him. He told the guy, "You're saved by the waitress."

I dug in as soon as I sat down, refusing to look up at him. He kept looking at me though, like I was a puzzle that needed solving. I watched the people as they line danced and slow danced and threw darts. After I finished what I could of the huge burger, I pushed it away and finally glanced up to find him studying me intently, his face indecisive.

I sighed and looked away. "I'm going to the bathroom. Do you mind getting me a diet to-go if she comes back?"

"No, I don't mind," he said and leaned back. He watched me cross the entire restaurant. I groaned once safe inside the girls' stalls. What had I been thinking? Now things were just going to be weird and he wasn't going to make things easy on me, obviously.

When I emerged from the bathroom, the first guy who asked me to dance was there. I smiled and waved as I passed, but he grabbed my arm. "Hold up."

I looked at the hand on my arm and up at him. "Yes?"

"You and that weirdo out there dating or something?"

"Why?"

"I saw you check in to the motel. Thought maybe you'd be here a while…"

I scoffed and yanked my arm away. "Yes. We're dating and completely head over feet."

"It looked like you were fighting out there, before that weird prancy, eighteenth century dancing."

Protectiveness rolled over me. "Don't knock on him just because he knows how to dance."

He smiled condescendingly. "I'll show you how to dance if that's what you want." He eyed the back door, which was right near the bathrooms. "But honestly, I'd rather get out of here."

"Well, have fun with that." I turned to go, but knew it wasn't going to be that easy. He grabbed my arm again.

"Well, just wait. I guarantee you if you give me a minute, I can talk you into going with me." He smiled. "I'm not such a bad guy. You just need to give ol' Landon a chance."

"You shouldn't have to talk people into going out with you. They should want to or not. And talking about yourself in the third person—weird, Landon."

His smiled faded. "You're one of them city girls, ain't you? Think they're better than everybody else."

"No, actually. Now excuse me."

I moved to leave and his grip on my arm tightened. I turned and snapped my hand into the back of his elbow, slamming him and his face into the wall. He was so shocked that he didn't even make a sound at the maneuver, just a small, "What the…"

"A couple years in the military at your service," I muttered. "Not a city girl."

He started to push back, his surprise gone, but I heard the commotion to my left. Before I could look Landon was yanked from my hands and dragged out the back door. I followed and found Enoch holding him with one hand to the brick wall as Landon gasped and grunted. Enoch was strong, I knew that; he wasn't human. He was feeding off of him right now, which was probably a good thing. The blue veins were back in full swing. I watched as they pulsed as if alive under his skin as he seethed looking up at the man who had asked me to dance.

Landon clawed at Enoch's arms, but he didn't budge. I went to his back, careful to keep my emotions in check. I couldn't be afraid right now. Enoch wouldn't hurt me. For goodness sake, he was doing this *for me*. "Enoch, let him go."

"He grabbed you. I saw him."

"Then you also saw me take care of things."

"Doesn't mean he doesn't deserve to pay for..." he shook his head as if he was wrestling with himself, "for thinking he has the right to touch you."

"I think he's going to remember this lesson for a very long time," I said and sighed looking up to Landon's eyes. They were as round as muscadines as he looked between me and Enoch. He nodded as much as he could and choked a word that I didn't understand. "Enoch," I pleaded. God, please don't let him kill this man.

Enoch lowered him slowly and got right in his face. "You do realize that her asking for me to release you in the *only* reason you're still alive?" He nodded. "Go," he boomed.

The man took off, tripping and clambering around the corner. I watched and then looked back at Enoch to find him right in my face. I gasped and put my hand on his chest out of reflex.

"Why must you keep..." He growled and lifted his fist. He was angry. At me? I looked up at him and didn't look away. He may be a coward, but in this moment, I wasn't going to be one. His breathing was so hard. "Why do you always get into these situations?" he finally boomed.

"I would have been fine," I answered quietly. "He was harmless."

"Harmless," he scoffed. "You didn't feel the lust coming off him like I did. He was not harmless. He was trying to lure you out!" he yelled. I backed away a little out of instinct. "He was trying to lure you away so he could hurt you. If you didn't cooperate, you don't think he would have forced you? I know his kind. I used to be his kind!" He kept coming and I kept retreating until I hit the wall and could go nowhere else. He kept getting louder and the blue veins were back, but I didn't know what I was doing to make him so angry. I watched as the blue rivers of anger crawled across his neck and arms, getting bigger and more vibrant by the second. Up this close, it was almost beautiful how colorful they were. "I know exactly what he wanted to do to you. And you, so gullible, just going to stand right by the bloody exit and let him do it? How stupid do you have to be? How many times do I have to save you before you get it that you have to start saving yourself?" I felt the first sob shake my chest as I stared into his violet eyes, but he was oblivious. "I can't wait to get there and finally be done with constantly watching over you." I just shut my eyes and turned my face, the sob rising in my throat, but he kept going. "You're just like Clara. Selfish. You don't care about whose life you're ruining by being in it, you just care about what you need and what you want." He pounded his fist on the brick wall by my head to accentuate his angry point. The tears fell from my eyes, but I just stayed right there. I wasn't scared. I knew he wasn't going to hurt me. He was just trying to get me to hate him, just like before. He didn't want to feel anything and didn't want me to either. He thought making me hate him would be easier because he wasn't a good guy.

Didn't he see how this was so much worse?

He sucked in few telling breaths that told me he knew I was upset. But he kept going, though some of his steam was gone. "You've got to think. There are forces bigger than us. You can't just...feel whatever you want. You can't just do whatever or go wherever... You can't just make people fall for you."

I opened my eyes and looked up at him, totally getting it then. He was angry that he learned I wanted him. But why would he care unless that meant he...

He was still so angry, the veins still standing out and vibrant against his pale skin, but he gently swiped under my eye with his thumb and sighed, stirring the hair at my temple.

"How are you not running screaming from me right now?"

My breathing was choppy, but I tried to make it steady. "I trust you."

He cursed and leaned close, his forehead pressed against mine. "Bloody hell, Fay. Don't make me fall for you," he whispered and I sucked in a breath.

"You hate me," I mused.

He chuckled, still sounding so angry, but opened his eyes and looked right into my soul. "I am so far away from hating you."

I couldn't help but laugh a little at that statement. It was a nervous, scoffing, strange sound. He leaned back just a smidge with a smile on his lips. The blue veins were almost all gone now. He sighed and surprised me by cupping my face. "He didn't hurt you, did he?"

I shook my head. "No."

He pressed his lips together and gently let my face go. "I saw almost the whole thing. You...did good."

"It didn't sound like I did good just now."

"Devourers are jealous, temperamental, biased, and jealous creatures."

I tried to hide my smile. "You said jealous twice."

"It deserves to be there twice." He grinned. "Don't piss off a devourer who has his sights on someone."

"Sights?" I asked, but didn't look at him as we walked back to the car. He didn't elaborate so I continued. "Okay, so devourers are jealous and temperamental." I met his eyes over the top of the car. "So what does any of that have to do with the fact that some random guy put his hands on me?"

A couple blue veins shivered in his neck. "Don't even say that," he growled. "And it has to do with the fact I don't hate you, princess. Get in."

I smiled and did as he asked. We drove the short distance across the lot to the hotel and got back out. I said I needed a shower and went to do just that. I washed my clothes in the sink since I'd been wearing them for two or three days now. I had lost count. I hung them on the rack and put the robe on, opting to sleep in that for the night. He eyed me when I came out. I hooked my thumb over my shoulder. "I had to wash my clothes. Hopefully they'll be dry by morning."

He didn't hide the fact that he was eyeing me, foot to head, his stare lingering on my legs and feet.

"You should turn in," he said gruffly and leaned his head back on the crummy chair, closing his eyes.

"Thanks for your help with that guy tonight, for what it's worth. Goodnight."

I flicked the light off by the bed and crawled under the covers. I heard him sigh and shift around. "You're welcome."

Six
Enoch

She was having a nightmare, but was almost awake. Her breathing was changing and I knew it was almost over. I wanted to wake her. I hated to feel her fear; it wasn't as bad feeding off her sorrow though and honestly, I needed to feed when I could. So I sat in the chair and soaked up her anxiety, hating every single second of it. I gripped my fists tighter on my thighs, hoping she would wake up soon.

But she kept right on dreaming. The longer she dreamt, the guiltier I felt. Finally, I could take it no longer and went to shake her awake. She gasped and grabbed my collar. Looking down into her eyes, I waited for her to understand that the dream was over and reality was here. Unless she had been dreaming about me and I was the monster. Then she would never wake up, would she?

But she sighed and pulled me down, hugging my neck. My entire body tightened out of reflex. I had never hugged anyone of my own accord, not even women I was trying to feed from. Hugging wasn't something that came with that. But she seemed to want it, need it even, so I let my elbow rest on the bed to hold me up and lifted a little to look at her. She was crying. "Ah, love, what's wrong?"

She smiled a little through her tears. "It's really cute when you say 'love'."

I lifted up and pulled her up with me, moving to the chair. She seemed a little taken aback when I put her in my lap, but sniffed and settled in. I rubbed her back and when she sighed, I sighed. There was something oddly satisfying about knowing she was contented. "Now. What's wrong? What was your dream about?"

"It's stupid," she muttered under her breath and rubbed her nose. That adorable little nose...

"It's not," my voice answered gruffly.

She looked up then, her eyes still wet. "Clara was in a big field and when I tried to walk toward her...she kept getting farther and farther away. When I yelled her name, she turned and ran, like she didn't want to see me."

"Sounds like someone is letting their fears rule their dreams."

She looked down and watched as my thumb passed over the hump of her knee, over and over. I hadn't even realized I was doing it. "I'm afraid she won't want to see me. I was awful to her."

"I was awful to my brother," I said and shrugged. "It's what siblings do."

"It's not that simple."

"Why don't we get there and see where you're at with her before we throw in the towel, yeah?"

She eyed me and cocked her head to the side. "You can be really sensible when you want to be."

"Sensible is my middle name."

She laughed softly at first and then picked up steam, leaning forward with no choice but to buckle into my chest.

"Hey, now," I said good-naturedly and poked her ribs.

She just laughed harder and it was too good to pass up when I realized how ridiculously ticklish she was. She tried to hold my hand down, but I was so much stronger than her. I let her see that, easily pushing her hands away and going in for the kill. "No, no, no," she begged and giggled.

Her face fell into my neck, the warm air puffing from her lips against my skin as she tried to catch her breath. The robe covered her body completely, but I could still feel her under the robe, her ribs under my hands. If she were the devourer in this situation, she'd be tasting my want right now. I couldn't help myself as I leaned my face closer, smelling her hair. Mmm, that shower of hers last night did wondrous things to her smell. She hit her fist against my shoulder, pressing it there, but then she stopped fighting me. I realized I had stopped tickling her and we were just staring at each other.

She licked her lips and was so close that when she breathed out of her parted lips, it hit my own exhale. I groaned, unable to help it. Her eyes widened a smidge, but she didn't back away. I waited for her fear to come, but it never did. Before I knew it, her want and yearning were mixing with my own.

I smoothed her cheek and found myself marveling at how this human was changing me. She wasn't just soft, she was soft-hearted and kind. I sighed heavily. "Do you feel better now?" I looked down and let my hand fall.

She surprised the hell out of me by picking my hand up and putting it back onto her cheek. "I do feel better, because of you. Thank you. Why do you do that?"

"Do what?" I asked with an astonished laugh, but still let my thumb coast across her cheekbone.

"Why do you always run? Act like…you don't feel anything?" She looked as though she wanted to turn away, embarrassed, but she was being brave. If she was going to be brave, then so could I be.

"Because I'm not good for anyone. It doesn't matter how much I might want you. It's not a good idea, Fay." She seemed surprised that I actually answered her question. "You asked." I quirked a small smile.

"I did." She leaned further into my touch and smiled a little. "You're not as bad as you think you are."

"You just don't know me," I said easily.

"Yet," she said, hard and steady, daring me to contradict her.

"Why do you want to?" I felt me brow lower in genuine curiosity. "You know I'm a monster, right?" I could hear my voice lowering in anger as I went on, but I tried to keep it steady. "I was made to be evil, Fay." I gritted my teeth, knowing how I laughed and scolded Eli for having this exact conversation with Clara. "Don't try to find goodness where there is none."

"Evil didn't save me when he could have walked away." I opened my mouth, but she pressed her fingers over my lips. "Evil didn't save me last night, either."

It was the first time I could remember ever wanting to be something else. I would have given anything to be good in that moment, to be someone worthy of her. I let myself have this small piece of time that would flit away into the nothingness when we reached her sister and Clara told her who I really was. Once she heard it from her sister's mouth, she wouldn't deny it any longer. She'd hate me then as Clara does. But for this moment, I just wanted to pretend that I could be what she needed. I took her face in my hands, knowing they were too rough against her soft skin.

She sat pliable and willing, waiting for me to make a move, to say something, anything. I didn't deserve that kind of devotion and adoration, especially not from Fay, but I still wanted to pretend. "I don't think I've ever met someone so soft."

"You've met a lot," she remarked evenly.

"I have. This is the first time in my life that I wish I hadn't." The surprise washed over her face and I continued. "But I am what I am. I'm not a good guy. I'm a demon who's messed up more times than I can remember. I eat fear, Fay." I shook my head, hoping she understood. She just watched me. "Will you please stop looking at me like that and say something."

"Looking at you like what?" she asked and her eyes fluttered a little when my fingers curled under chin.

"Like you don't believe that I'm evil. Like you think I'm savable."

"*I* know you are. It's just a matter of getting *you* to see it." She moved her hands to my chest and this was bad. This was so bad.

We were just feeding off each other's energy at this point, no pun intended. We barely knew each other, but being stuck together these past few days and all the talking we'd done had brought us closer than I had wanted. And when you save someone, they get a hero complex sometimes. Well, I saved her several times. She was attracted to me. I had so many variables working against me. There was no way she wanted me for just me. How could she? It was this devourer's body and what I was made to do, drawing her in. The one time I didn't want to snatch up a female and I couldn't seem to stop wanting to reel her in.

"Fay," I said, but it was more of a growl. She smiled, but it was so genuine and willing it made my chest ache. "Fay, don't. It's just an illusion to trick you, to make you trust us and believe that you're safe when you're anything but."

I went to scoot her up, but she gripped tighter to my shoulders. "I'm sure that most devourers are that way. And I'm sure you used to be that way. You told me so. You've told me the truth the entire time, not even sparing my feeling," she scoffed. "When someone wants to change or goes through something that makes them different...it doesn't matter what they were, it only matters what they want to be."

I let my thumbs caress her cheeks and balked at that revelation. "It can't really be that simple to humans, can it?"

"Why not?"

"Because the rest of the world is anything but."

She squirmed a little, settling more on my lap. I held in my groan just barely before she asked, "We'll be there today, won't we?"

"Yes," I whispered. "And then the illusions you have of me will be over." I let my hands fall to my lap and patted her sides, trying for a smile. "Clara will be sure to set you straight about me, don't worry."

"I'm the older sister," she insisted and finally lifted herself from my lap. I felt her absence as a relief and a burden at the same time. "I'll handle her. I just really want to see her." She smiled, but looked as if she could cry, too.

"Well, go get dressed. Today will be...interesting." I wasn't sure if I needed to find a witch's stone to get into the camp or not. "I need you to keep an open mind." I got up and looked in her eyes, holding her chin. "I need you to stay calm and just follow my lead. I'll keep you safe and I'll get you there. You'll see some things that won't be normal, but you'll be okay."

She smiled, looking a little dazed like they usually did and I hated myself for using persuasion on her, but knew it was best. "Okay, Enoch."

"Okay, Fay."

She smiled, back to herself so quickly. "I kinda like it when you say my name with your accent."

"Most women do," I said sarcastically and leaned back against the wall. She stopped and looked back, noticing my tone. I waved her off. "Nothing, princess. Let's get going."

She nodded, but I could tell that she hated the thought she'd insulted me somehow. I wiped my face with my hands. How was I going to survive this human girl who was turning me into such a pansy?

Once we got dressed and on the road, I told her we'd stop in between breakfast and lunch for something to eat if that was fine.

It seemed like all we did was stop and cater to her human needs in some form or another. I was growing tired of the anxiousness building in my gut. Ready to find Eli and the rebels, I wanted to get there as quickly as possible. Rebels being what they were, they didn't have any phones or cells. Fay said the last thing she had from Clara was a letter telling her where she was going, but she hadn't heard from here since. That was months ago right after the wedding.

"She's not ignoring you," I told her, "they just don't have any phones where they are."

"How is that possible? Everyone has phones."

"Not idiots who join groups who move to the middle of nowhere and take up arms for the greater good," I mumbled under my breath.

"I heard that," she hissed and turned in her seat. I rolled my eyes and kicked myself. "What the hell are you talking about?"

"Nothing."

"No, not this *nothing* stuff. You don't get to blow me off—"

"I can," I insisted. "Now let me drive in peace."

She huffed. "Don't start being grumpy Enoch again. Do you need to feed again already?"

I glared at her for longer than I should have. "Really?"

"Watch the road!" She leaned over in my lap and grabbed the wheel. "Enoch, don't be a lunatic," she scolded as she leaned back in her seat.

"I'm only a lunatic when it comes to you it," I groaned my annoyance. But for some strange reason, she took that as a compliment. Her cheeks bloomed and her fingers fidgeted as her lips opened. I stopped her by interrupting with, "And don't even try to cover that up, princess."

She huffed a surprised breath, as if she didn't know what to do next. "I don't know what to do with you sometimes, Enoch."

I grinned. "I can think of a few fun things." I looked over, expecting to see a smile at my goading, but she wasn't smiling. She was doing the opposite of smiling and it made me want to crawl into a hole.

"Like right now," she admitted and turned to look out the window. "I don't know what to do with you. I can't tell if you're real or not."

"What do you mean?" I asked quickly, not letting the moment simmer for fear that I'd chicken out.

"I know you did something to me." She lifted her legs up on the seat, rested her chin on her knee, and looked over. "I feel so okay with everything and that doesn't make any real sense." She looked right in my eyes. "Are you going to deny it?"

I shook my head, glancing between her and the road. "No. I persuaded you to be accepting of the things going on, to protect your mind and sanity, so I could get you to your sister safely and quickly."

"And that's all?" she asked and there seemed to be an underlying question she wasn't asking. I felt my brow lower in question. "You didn't add anything else in there, some other addendum or agenda?"

I shook my head, knowing that she no longer trusted me, no longer cared, and no longer wanted me to be near her. The afterglow was over. The short-lived dream I had of living some normal life was done. I had been stupid to think it could be true for even a morning.

"No, Fay," I said and stared at the road as steadily as I could muster, but it still came out gravely and tortured. "No, I just wanted to help you."

She turned to look at my profile, but I didn't look back at her. I drove a little faster than I should have, determined to get there faster. She didn't want to be here with me any longer than necessary, not anymore anyway.

To find to a tortured soul, just follow the road littered with his own transgressions.

She fell asleep not long after that, slumped against her seat, but her face wasn't peaceful. I felt guilt in my throat like a lump, pressing against me, not letting me breathe or think. I hated it. I'd never felt guilt until that girl in the alley and now this girl was bringing me to my knees with it. I took her legs and brought them into my lap. She leaned back and stretched out, wiggling to get comfortable. When she sighed, my very soul sighed with her.

I hated it and loved it and prayed it would stop and would never go away. I drove the rest of the way with that aggravating, precious female's feet in my lap and my mind in tumbles.

———

We were so close, but I knew she was going to need to eat. I pulled into the restaurant off the interstate, our last stop for the day, and woke her gently, my hand brushing her knee. She woke as she always did—little moans and noises as she arched and pushed her chest up in stretches that would make any man insane. I averted my gaze to be honorable, because I'd done enough damage, but that was the absolute only reason. Otherwise the view was magnificent and could be watched for hours on end. I groaned a little and leaned my head back on the seat, pressing my fingers into my eyes.

She pulled her feet from my lap and I hissed. She gasped and halted before her breathing sped up noticeably.

"I wasn't trying to take over the whole car. Sorry." She pulled her feet away and put her shoes back on. She wasn't looking at me and I didn't blame her.

I was stacking up winning points left and right, wasn't I? Did it even matter? I didn't really want this girl, did I? Even after the insane conversation last night in alley where I had practically said that I did? And this morning?

I opened my door, practically jumped from the car, and slammed it before I started analyzing my own questions. She got out and seemed puzzled with my outburst. She came to my side, but kept her distance. "Are we close?"

"What?" I asked, but it was a gruff growl.

She sighed and seemed even more disappointed. "Are we close? To Clara?"

"Oh. Yeah, a couple hours."

"Good," she answered and sighed again, licking her lips. "Then you'll be able to get rid of me," she muttered as she walked off.

I didn't even try to refute her words. There was no point. I was disappointing her left and right, and anything I said would just sound like I was lying or trying to cover. I just needed to get her there. If I could keep my promise to her and get her to her sister, then I could remove the persuasion and go from there. But until then, I just felt like a bastard no matter what I did.

The place was crawling with country bumpkins. The hostess almost got a throat punch when she shouted, "Howdy, folks! Welcome to Cracker Barrel."

"Um, howdy." Fay looked back with a peculiarly intrigued look and smiled. "Two, please."

As we followed her to the table past a roaring fire and people playing checkers, I leaned forward and whispered, "This place is strange."

"I would think it would be right up your alley."

"Why?" I asked wryly and looked around at the black and white pictures of people. She gave me a coy smile. "Because I'm old?"

"That's one way of looking at it."

"You don't look old to me," the older, plump waitress said and slammed some waters on the table. "What'll you have?"

"What do you suggest?"

"The meatloaf is divine."

"I somehow doubt that," I remarked, which earned me a kick from under the table, "but I'll take a shot in the dark. Why not."

"I'll have the same, please, with the mashed potatoes and mac-n-cheese."

"Same," I remarked and handed her our menus.

"Can I just say how much I love your accent? I bet you hear that all the time," she said and smiled as she waited for some charming reply.

I looked at Fay and smirked as I told the waitress, "You're the first, sweetheart."

She left with a giggle, her wrinkled cheeks rosy and eyes shining as she scooted away. Fay stared at me for so long that I started to wonder if I'd once again done something wrong. The woman was old. Fay had to know there was no competition there. And then I remembered that Fay hated me now and wanted nothing to do with me. So it couldn't be that.

"What, Fay?" I finally asked, my voice so soft and low I barely heard it. But *she* heard it. "What have I done now?"

"You made her night just now. Do you know that?"

I scoffed with a smile. "She's a sweet old lady stuck in a crappy job. Nothing wrong with making her feel young a bit."

"And that's exactly what I mean." She leaned on the table to be closer to be me. "But you didn't have to do that. You could have just let her walk away and not said a word. But instead, you, Enoch," her voice cracked like she might cry and I was so confused, "made an old woman try to have a good night. You're amazing sometimes."

I stared into those gorgeous green eyes of hers and brought my hand up to cup her chin, letting my thumb brush over her jaw. "Fay…I don't know what you want from me," I said softly. "And even if I did, I don't know if I could give it to you."

"Neither do I," she replied just as softly and wrapped her hand around my wrist. "I don't know anything anymore."

"Ah," I said in understanding and leaned back. "And that's my fault, is it?"

"Is it? You put the persuasion on me. I don't know what's real anymore. I don't know if what I…feel is real."

I got it. I shook my head. She thought I made her feelings for me out of thin air, that they were fabricated and not real. I opened my mouth to tell her that I hadn't done that when there was a noise behind me. I turned to see the commotion when I saw our waitress running from the kitchen. The terrified look on her face told me all I needed to know. The Horde had found us.

I gripped Fay's hand and took off toward the back door, shoving her in front of me to shield her. "What about those people?" she asked in a shriek.

"I don't care about them, I care about you."

She yanked her arm away from me and stared up at me in the middle of the parking lot. I went to grab her again and she moved away. "Fay," I growled.

"Enoch, those people are going to be hurt, or worse, because of us."

"Not us," I made the epic mistake of saying with a scoff. Her lips parted and she looked hurt more than appalled. "Fay," I sighed her name and wanted to just throw her over my shoulder and drag her away. The old me would have done just that. I tightened my fist as I watched her back away toward the door of the restaurant, feeling the old feelings bubbling up in me. Why shouldn't I? She'd be mad, but she'd eventually forgive me.

I pressed my lips in a thin line and blurred to her, but when I reached her, something in her face made me change my mind. Instead of lifting her, I just stood there. She must have known what had been on my mind though, because the determination on her face was evident.

"Don't you dare," she begged. She didn't order me, she begged, knowing that I was stronger and could make her if I really wanted to. "Please, Enoch. They didn't do anything wrong but come into work and go out to lunch and go about their day as usual." I heard the door open and knew they were coming. Our time had run out. She knew it, too, and her eyes danced between my eyes and the restaurant. "I know I ask a lot of you, but it's not too much."

I laughed once without humor. "It is though. In every scenario of this trip, you've asked me to go against what I am, what I was made to do. It's not natural. A devourer doesn't save people and run around being the hero."

She didn't smile as she put her hand on my cheek and pressed her chest to mine. "You've been my hero since I met you. And I never once asked you to save me. You did that all on your own."

I swallowed, my mouth felt dry and useless. "Fay," I groaned—a plea. She was murdering the man I used to be with her acceptance. It didn't make any sense for her to be so kind and generous to me when I did nothing to deserve it.

I looked at the restaurant. I could hear them and knew from the noises I heard that there were about ten men present. "Stay here."

"No way. I'm—"

"You're staying." I glared at her and dared her to argue. "If I'm going in there and doing this for you, then I'm doing it my way." She sighed, relieved, and then she tensed and seemed upset for an entirely new reason. I groaned. "I can't keep up with you. I can't seem to make you happy no matter what I do."

"I just didn't think it through. I don't want them to get hurt for us," she yelled quickly. "But you..." Her gaze bounced back and forth. "I don't want to lose you either."

"Lose me?" I bent down to find her line of sight. "How would you lose me?"

"You can die, can't you?" she asked angrily.

"Hardly. It's very hard to kill a devourer. Especially since I have the advantage and know that they're here."

She sighed harshly and gripped her shirt over her heart. "Really?"

"Yes, really." I put the keys in her palm and gave her what I hoped was a stern look. "You leave that car and I'll..." I gulped and said, "I'll be very angry with you, Fay."

"I won't," she promised breathily and stared, hesitating, before she reached around my neck and gripped tightly.

My hands went straight to her perfect hips. I groaned in my mind and was shocked that it hadn't come out of my mouth, needing an outlet. "I need to go," I said into her hair. "We need to get back on the road as soon as possible. They'll try to stop us from reaching the camp, so we need to hurry."

"Okay," she mumbled against my shoulder. She leaned back and looked up at me. "Be careful." It wasn't a request.

I nodded and walked backward to watch her climb in the car and lock the door before I turned to sprint to the back door of the restaurant. I took out the one who was keeping watch out the back door, and doing an appalling job. I snapped his neck before he even knew I was there.

When I opened the door slowly and peeked in, I saw they had herded most of the workers and diners into the back and were questioning them one by one. They didn't seem to be hurting them. I tapped the one in the back on the shoulder and nodded my head at him. He got the attention of the others and they all filed out single file, quietly. I shook my head at how idiotically easy that had been.

I inched forward toward the men asking the questions and listened in as they showed them pictures and asked if they'd seen us. I cursed under my breath when I realized the person left behind was our fragile old waitress. If it had been anyone else, I'd had left and been happy that we saved all those people, but I wouldn't leave her. I waited until things quieted and I knew that she was only in the room with one or two men and then moved in. When I moved in, I grimaced at being wrong.

There were still four men in with her and they were looking at a local map they'd gotten from the shop, trying to see the best route—figuring which route we would've taken out of there. They hadn't even known we were there at all until that moment. I saw it all over their faces. We were free and clear outside, but I had let Fay give me a conscience about these people; I had let her make me feel bad about these people, otherwise, we would have been home free.

"Well, well—"

I blurred forward and throat punched him. "Let's skip the introductions." I reached over and grabbed a knife from the counter and slung it right to the next guy, spearing it through his hand, tacking him to the wall. I heard a scream that was definitely human. I looked at my waitress' nametag and moved toward her. "Pamela. It's all right. I came back to make sure everyone was okay."

"I'm not okay! You stabbed him!"

"In all fairness, he was going to stab me first."

Her eyes moved to my right and her mouth opened. I turned just as she said, "Watch out!"

I cracked his neck and she squealed like a stuck pig. "Pamela, please," I said calmly and I stared down my last opponent.

A rolling pin was tossed over my shoulder and I smiled at her. "Thanks, sweetheart, but that won't really help on his kind." The guy with the knife through his hand was now free also and they were both coming for us. "Or him."

"His kind?" she asked as she gripped the back of my shirt tightly. "What does that mean?"

"It means run, Pamela."

"But…I saw you," she whispered. Like whispering somehow made it less real. "I saw you move way too fast to be…normal. What's going on?" She sobbed a quick, short breath. "Please. I just want to see my grandkids again."

I looked at her over my shoulder and felt her fear smack into me. I tried not to groan. "Pamela," I said slowly, "I'll take care of this." I smiled as best I could. "I'm sorry that you came into work today thinking it was going to be a normal day. Look at me." I waited for her eyes to meet mine. "You go—go and see your grandkids and don't worry about what's going on here. It's not important. Be safe and be…happy."

She walked backward and watched me as she left. She stopped at the door and I didn't understand. I persuaded her to go. She should want to leave and go—

"Thank you. Thank you for what you did. I know you're not…normal. I know something isn't right here and you could've very well not come back for us. Thank you for doing that. My grandbabies thank you." She sobbed as she turned to go and took off in a run.

I turned my full attention to the devourers and they were completely stunned. "What in the hell…is wrong with you, Enoch Thames?"

I charged. I knocked their heads together before grabbing a handful of hair from each and wrenching as hard as I could. I heard the sickening snap of both of their necks. It didn't make me feel good or bad that I enjoyed it. It just was what it was. I was a devourer and no matter how much I changed, there were some things that wouldn't. Like the fact that taking out my enemy— the people who had tried to hurt me, Fay, and an old woman that didn't deserve it—would always bring satisfaction.

I knew they'd be awake soon enough so I turned to go, but saw something on the counter that made me pause. I smiled.

When I made it back to the car a couple minutes later, I could see that Fay was working herself into a tizzy. She unlocked the door when she saw me coming and smiled at what I was holding. "Ah, I think I just fell in love with you."

I cut my eyes at her as I climbed in and she rolled hers. "You know what I mean." She took one of the to-go plates and opened it up. "Oh, my gosh. Pancakes."

"And I got eggs and bacon. All they had cooked and ready to go was breakfast stuff."

"It doesn't matter. I'm starving," she said and dipped her pancake into the syrup, taking a big bite and smiling at me, licking her lip and laughing when it dripped on her chin. She didn't even care that it was making a mess. It was adorable and cute, but most women I'd known were so self-conscious about it. She seemed to…relish in it.

She sat in the middle instead of in her seat on the far side and when she was done she laid her head on my shoulder. I tried not to be too excited about that.

"Thank you for going back in there. I know you didn't want to, and I appreciate that you did it." Her hair smelled like that hotel shampoo. I would forever love that smell for the rest of my days. I gulped when I felt her fingers lightly touch my arm. "I can't believe we're almost there."

I coughed. "Yeah. Our trip is almost over. You're almost rid of me."

"You're not going to leave, are you?" She sat up and scooted a little closer, her leg propped up in the seat with her touching my arm. "He's your brother, too. There's no reason for you to just rush off and leave, is there?"

"Clara hates me."

She scoffed. "That can't really be true."

"I hate her."

She sighed and looked at me. "You have these moments where you're so...amazing." My heart actually hurt it jumped so violently. "And then you have these other moments where I question everything that's ever happened between us."

I swallowed. "You should."

"Why?" she breathed.

"I'm a devourer."

"You saved me," she argued, as if that argument meant something to top all other arguments.

I finally glanced over and wished I hadn't. She was waiting for me to say something epic. "I'm not good for you."

She sighed like she was disappointed. "So you're going to leave once we're there. You're just going to drop me off?"

"I'll stay for a bit, but not for long. It's not for me. I'm a loner. That's always been my life."

"Because you choose it."

"Yes," I sighed. "Because I choose it."

"You could choose something else."

Was she really asking me to choose her? She barely knew me and the little bit she did know wasn't good. She couldn't want me in that way from what she'd seen...could she?

The rest of the trip was silent. She brooded and I wanted to be angry about it, but it was the cutest thing I'd ever laid eyes on. She was angry that I was leaving. I had never had someone care about my being *there*. I could have kissed her for that alone.

The next part of the trip was tricky.

I knew the general vicinity of where Clara and Eli were, but I knew it wasn't going to be that easy to get in. They moved around so much, and I didn't know if they were going to be hidden with some magic. If they were, I was going to have to find a witch to find them. I sighed. So close, but still so far away. And there was no way to reach them.

And I was already beginning to feel the need to feed again. The twitchiness in my veins and blood. I shook my head, knowing that it wasn't going to make anything easier. The next hour I beat a rhythm on the steering wheel and tried to think of what Eli would do if it was him making the decisions for the rebels. And then I tried to think of where Franz would take them. When we reached the last known place, it was empty, they were already gone, and I felt my anger rise even as Fay's hope fell.

"I was stupid to think it would be that easy, huh?" She sniffed a laugh. "I don't deserve to find her. She probably doesn't even want me to. If she knew I was looking for her, she's probably run anyway."

"We'll find them," I insisted. "I figured they'd moved. They're practically gypsies. It's how they live."

She watched me, her green eyes following me as I looked around the campsites, looking for clues. She was getting madder by the second as she watched me pick up things and toss them away as is they didn't matter. "Don't tell me things just to make me feel better," she sneered.

I laughed and gave her a look. "I am the last person who would sugarcoat it for you, sweetheart."

She looked at the ground, letting her breath that she was holding go, knowing I was right. "I shouldn't have gotten my hopes up. That was just stupid." I passed behind her when I moved to search near the river and heard her mutter, "And will you stop calling me *sweetheart?*"

I raised an eyebrow. "Sweetheart is offensive? Since when?"

She steeled herself, lifting her chin and straightening her back. She reminded me of Clara so much right then. "You're not going to do anything about it. Since you decided you're leaving, dumping me as soon as you find them, you don't get to *sweetheart* me." She crossed her arms, turned away from me, and walked toward one of the only small cabins that was there and I stared, stunned.

Any other time and I would have been so turned on by that little speech and the fact that this female was coming on to me, but this was Clara's sister. I squeezed my eyes shut and clenched my fists. Why? Why, why, why?

My life was practically in shambles and I certainly didn't need a female added to the mix to keep things interesting right now. So why was I going so crazy over this one?

"They're gone. I can't find anything left behind to lead us to them." I looked back to find her wiping her eyes and taking a deep breath as she tried to compose herself by the river bank. "I'm sorry, Fay. We need to go."

"It's so beautiful here," she mused and sighed long and hard. She leaned her head back and rolled her neck to the side, her eyes closed. She was so trusting. I realized how completely she trusted me on every level. No matter what happened, I had to get this girl to Clara. I rubbed her arm with my thumb and she didn't flinch like I thought she would. She smiled and grabbed my arm, linking hers with mine. "Just come here for a minute."

I sighed. "Fay."

"Just a second. Everybody needs to recharge every once in a while. And you, sir, need to recharge more than most people."

"I take offense to that," I spouted back.

She giggled and that giggle almost did me in, with her eyes closed and her still so completely trusting me. "Just close your eyes and lean your head back. Soak up the sun for a second and listen to the water."

"Devourers don't like sun. Or the sound of the river."

"That's a lie and you know it." She smiled.

"How do you know that?" I groaned.

"Because. That would just be crazy," she said softly. She leaned her head on my shoulder and we probably sat there for a full ten minutes without moving, just listening. She lifted her head and looked at me. She bit her lip on the side and I wanted to be the one biting that lip. "So, do you feel better?"

"Truth?" She nodded. "I do actually. I mean. I don't feel physically better, and I still need to feed, but…just sitting here with you somehow…"

"It's scientific," she corrected. I squinted. "Vitamin D absorbs in your skin and releases endorphins in your body that do all sorts of good things for you. Improves your mood, for one."

"Endorphins?" I questioned and smirked. "I thought endorphins made you sexually charged—"

She slapped my chest, rolled her eyes, turned toward the car. "Way to ruin my good mood, Enoch."

I laughed my words, "What? You stated some facts, so I stated some facts."

"Facts, my behind!" I could hear the smile in her voice. I walked after her, her lovely rear right in my line of sight. She set me up so nicely for that one, now hadn't she?

"And what a gorgeous behind it is."

She turned, her mouth open to blast me one, but bumped into my chest instead because I had been so close. She put her hand on my chest and tried to retreat, but I had the advantage on this and wasn't in a giving mood if this was what it entailed. I came for her harder, but she kept her hand there even as she protested. "I thought we talked about this and you weren't going to...to..."

"To what...sweetheart?"

"That!" she shrieked and looked up at me like I was a villain. A villain with something she wanted. "The *sweethearts* and the *gorgeous behinds* and that stuff you're pulling on me. Stop it."

"But you don't like me. So why does it matter? I'm just trying to kill some time."

"I..." She licked her lips. "I never said I didn't like you."

I moved until she was pressed against me, her hand stuck between us. She was breathing hard and she made this little noise, a cross between a beg and a groan.

"Enoch," she tacked on with it and I was about to lose it.

I growled. "You are the most—"

We heard a loud, thunderous screech that sounded like a car accident from the road. We both jerked our gazes to the road and then back to each other. She opened her mouth and paused for only a second before asking, "I am the most what?"

I chuckled. "Looks like I was saved by the bell. Come on, princess. Maybe I'll tell you later."

She huffed and hung on to my hand as I tugged her up the steep hill back to the car. The pine needles made the climb slippery and hazardous.

When we reached the top of the hill, the car we'd stolen was gone. I blurred across the street, startling her with my quickness. I groaned. "A car doesn't just disappear," I bellowed. "We heard that noise. What the hell happened?"

"You should know better than to leave your getaway car in broad daylight, Thames."

I sighed and turned toward the further south side of the woods. "Franz."

He smiled. "Enoch." He turned to Fay and nodded his head once. "Miss."

"Fay," she said softly.

"Well, Fay. Any friend of Enoch's is a friend of the rebels'."

"You're here?" I questioned and blurred to Fay's side. She hadn't moved an inch and as soon as I got a taste of her fear, I moved without even thinking. I took her hand in mine and looked at her before tugging her to follow me, silently telling her it was okay. Franz watched the exchange and, even though he kept his expression the same, I could tell he was shocked. He didn't move or say a word for far too long as he studied me.

"Is something wrong?" Fay finally asked.

"Yes," Franz said and stared me down. "But we'll talk about that later." He smiled at her. "I'm sure you must be starving."

"Not really, actually. We ate not too long ago. But thank you," she rushed to say. "I really appreciate it, but Enoch has been doing a really good job of taking care of me."

Franz's eyes bulged. I sighed. "Has he now. Well." He left it at that and turned, we assumed for us to follow him.

She gripped my hand tighter and leaned in. "I think he was just expecting *you* to come. I don't think he's very happy about my just showing up out of nowhere."

"No," I assured. "No, it's not that."

"He didn't seem to like me being here very much."

I rubbed her fingers with mine and she shivered, causing a delicious ache to settle in my chest. I groaned. "You're killing me, little human."

"What?" she whispered.

I ignored that. "He's trying to figure me out. That's all. It's me, not you. I told you that I used to be different. The last time I saw them was months ago and I used to be…" I chuckled with the irony of it, "a lot different. I was an ass, Fay. I wasn't a good guy. I'm still not." I sighed, unable to hold it in. I lifted the hand that wasn't attached to her. "He knows me. He's known me for a very long time. They're all going to wonder what happened to me."

"So just tell them you changed. People change," she reasoned.

"Devourers aren't people, and devourers don't change," I argued softly. I stared at the green grass. I could hear Franz's steps stop as he waited for us. He couldn't hear us talking, but he knew that we were and he was waiting for us to finish. "They aren't going to believe me." I knew it was true. "They aren't going to believe that I've changed. They'll think I'm fooling around or playing some game."

"To what end?" she asked harshly, angry for me and we hadn't even been questioned yet. "Why would they think that?"

"You don't know the person I used to be, Fay. I was a bastard. I deserve every bit of menace coming my way. I've given enough of it myself, enough harm, enough hurt." I shook my head, hating the way she still looked at me with such hope. "I know you think there could be a future for us, but—"

"But you don't want one." She nodded. "You've made that perfectly and repeatedly clear."

"That's not what I mean."

"You've said you're leaving the second you get a chance." She pulled her hand away gently and let her eyes fall to the ground. "Thank you for saving me. I wouldn't be here if you hadn't. So thanks. I owe Clara. I need to see her even if she doesn't want to see me, so… I know you think you're this awful guy, but you did this great thing for me." She was biting her lip when her blue eyes met mine again. She looked like she might cry at any minute. I opened my mouth, but she seemed to think it would have been a bad idea for me to speak. She sprinted to catch up with Franz and started to ask him questions. Silly, nonstop questions.

She was just trying to keep him talking. I groaned and walked faster to catch up. He was telling her that they made the campsite to look as though they had come and gone so people would think they'd left already and wouldn't stick around. It was pretty clever because it had fooled even me. But on the other side of the river was another campsite.

"There is a way through the woods around the river, but it's loud and long and tedious. You can really only get there by boat," he was saying as he huffed a breath and led the way down a steep hill to the bank, "so it stays pretty quiet. We don't have to worry about any surprise visits."

"You mean like this," I replied wryly.

"With you it's always a surprise, Enoch." He gave me an equally wry smile as we reached the boats and he handed me the tie-off rope. "Here. Make yourself useful, Thames, and hold this while I help the lady in."

I growled an aggravated breath as he lifted her into the boat, one arm behind her back and one behind her knees, while she giggled and laughed. "Why, thank you, kind sir."

"Always willing to help a damsel in distress."

"That must be a running theme in these parts," she said and smiled in my direction.

Franz gave me a puzzled look with a following look that said he was about to ask a million questions, so I nipped that in the bloody bud. "So how is ol' Elijah doing?"

He smiled. "Oh, just fine. He and Clara are settling into the rebels smashingly."

"Clara?" Fay breathed. "You know Clara?"

"Yes," Franz asked and tensed. "Do you?"

"Franz," I eased and shook my head at him. He was always on full alert as the leader of the rebels. "This is Fay. Clara's sister."

He smiled, sitting at the back of the boat and pulled the cord to crank the old boat engine. "Nice to meet you, Clara's sister," he yelled over the roar. "Why don't you have a seat and hang on tight, sweetheart. I'm going to get you to Clara lickety-split."

I pulled her to my side and put my arm around her stomach to keep her down tight and safe. She shivered again in my grasp and my eyes rolled in my head. It took all I had not to groan.

Slowly she looked at me over her shoulder and her lips parted. My fist tightened on her stomach. I was about to haul her into my lap if she didn't stop being so unbelievably sexy.

I leaned forward a little and heard her breath catch, her chest lifted with the movement. My lips lifted with a smile. I pressed my lips to her ear and cupped her cheek and jaw to make absolute sure she heard me. "You. Are. Killing. Me."

The shivers practically assaulted her, but she leaned back just enough to see my face. If we weren't in a boat, I knew our breaths would be colliding in between us. It was a crime that I was being robbed of that.

"Little human?" she finished. I didn't hear it because she whispered it, but I saw her lips move.

I smiled, but didn't answer her. When she smiled back, I'd never wanted to kiss a human so badly in my entire life. I was actually pretty surprised that I'd been able to restrain myself this entire time with her. She was pretty kissable. When my thumb swept across her cheekbone, she closed her eyes like it was too much pleasure.

Where did this girl come from?

That's it. She was getting kissed. She deserved it, even if I didn't, but before I could really put any action to that thought, Franz was telling us to hang on and was docking us to the river bank. I stood and held my hand out, helping Fay out of the boat.

But as soon as I saw the group of people coming, I knew that everything was about to change for me. Even as Fay turned to say thank you and smile at me, I knew it wouldn't last. As soon as her sister saw me, it was all over. As soon as Clara told her what she really thought of me, she wouldn't look at me like a hero anymore.

She'd look at me like that bastard I really was.

Seven
Fay

I searched the people who were coming to see us. I hadn't seen her yet, but I knew I would and I knew it would be soon. Enoch was already acting strange, which I got. He said he was different and he thought people weren't going to understand. Or maybe he had done some things and he was worried that he wasn't going to be forgiven. Maybe that was it.

Either way, I was just ready to see her.

"Franz, can you go and get Clara for Fay?"

"What about you?" Franz asked him. I didn't know what that meant—get Eli, I guessed.

He shook his head. "Later. For now, just let her see her sister." He looked down at me. "I'm going to go take a walk."

I sighed, knowing it was all coming to a screeching halt. "Why? What's wrong?"

"Nothing," he said, his voice gruff. He groaned, making it worse. "I just don't want to be here right now, okay? You go see Clara. I got you here, didn't I? Just like I promised. So let me have some peace."

"If they can't see that you've changed, then screw them, Enoch."

He laughed humorlessly. "It doesn't work that way. Besides, it's like I told you—devourers don't just change like that. It means something and it's not good." He walked backward. "Just leave me alone for a while. You got what you wanted. You're here. Be happy about it." He smiled to take the sting away, but I saw right through it.

"Why are you being like this now that we're here?" Someone walked up to me and said hello, said their name and asked for mine, but I was still focused on Enoch as he walked away. "Enoch!"

He kept walking and didn't look. I looked at the guy who was speaking and tried to smile for him, but it was pointless. Enoch had taken the smile right off my face for the day and I was pathetic for letting him. But we had taken this journey together, hadn't we? I didn't know what kind of person, or devourer, he used to be. I know he wasn't human. I mean he made people have emotions so he could feed so I could imagine the kind of person that would make him.

But he was different now.

I didn't know what to think. Were all my thoughts about him because of his persuasion?

I said my hellos to the people who met me at the bank as I searched the faces one after another for a dark haired beauty that looked like my sister. And then there she was. Franz was next to her…and so was Enoch. I was so confused. He was giving me whiplash. Why was he being so confusing!

I ran to her.

She ran, too, and we met in the middle of the sea of people in a tangle of arms. People could tell there was a real reunion going on, so some clapping was going on and some "*awws*".

I hugged her so hard and noticed how hard she was hugging me back. We had always been the exact same height even though I was a couple years older. I smoothed her hair and found myself to be a blubbering mess in a matter of seconds. I covered my eyes with my hand around her head, but I just couldn't seem to stop crying. I finally pulled back and looked at her face. She seemed shocked. Beyond shocked. And that was all my fault.

"Clara, please forgive me."

I yanked her back to me and continued to squeeze her hard. She rubbed my back and gripped my shirt in her fingers. I thought she was just consoling me, but I felt wetness on my neck. I leaned back and held her face. Her cheeks were soaked, but she was so still. "I'm sorry," I told her. "I wasn't trying to upset you. I just—"

"I thought I'd never see you again." She smiled and cupped my face, too. "And then here you are, searching the country for me. I didn't think…you wanted to see me."

"And that was my fault. I'm a stupid girl. I'm sorry. Can you ever, ever forgive me for," I choked on a sob, "leaving you? Not being your sister when I should have been your sister the most?"

Her face crumpled. "Fay, I missed you so much."

I looked over at Enoch and smiled. "Changed your mind, huh?"

He squinted and smiled. "Uh…"

I moved to hug him around his waist and sighed at his warmth. "Look," I whispered. "It'll all be okay. People change and so can you. I think maybe you're not giving people enough credit." I leaned back to look at him and he was smiling at me, but it was this really cute, uncomfortable way.

I sighed. "Fine." I started to move back but behind us in the woods, coming towards us, was…Enoch. I looked up at his face and over at the one walking towards us. The one I had my arms around caught on and looked back. He tensed and then sighed. "Oh." He looked over at me as I moved away. "You thought I was Enoch."

"You're not Enoch?" I said, stating the glaringly obvious.

"You thought he was Enoch?" Clara screeched. "And you were hugging him? Why? How do you even know him?"

"He brought me here," I muttered, still not removing my eyes from the man who shared a face with Enoch. It was eerie and creepy and completely embarrassing that I'd just been hugging him. But now I could see he was different, yet the same. They were identical, like *identical*, but Eli had a little eyebrow piercing. And his clothes were obviously different now that I was paying attention.

"Sorry. I'm Eli." He held his hand out. "Enoch's twin brother. Clara's husband."

"Yeah, sorry," Clara spouted, "but manners go out the window when you talk about hugging the spawn of Satan."

Wow, Enoch wasn't kidding. Clara did hate him. He was almost here so I was going to nip this in the bud before he was within ear shot. "Clara, he brought me here. He saved my life."

She gasped. "More times than I can count. And he didn't have to. I didn't beg him. He did it out of nowhere before he even knew who I was, so lay off the *Enoch is evil* crap. He's changed. Like really changed. I'm sure he doesn't really want to hear it, and I for sure don't."

"That's all right, Fay," I heard so close in my ear that I had to hold in the shiver. So much for him being out of ear shot. "You don't have to fight my battles for me, but I appreciate it." I felt his warm palm on the inside of my wrist. I waited and prayed he would slide it down to connect it to my hand, palm to palm, but he didn't. "Eli."

"Brother. You came back. I didn't think you would."

Enoch moved away from me and put his hand on Eli's shoulder. "We...have a lot to talk about." He looked over. "Clara."

She looked at me and reached over, taking my hand. "Take off the persuasion, Enoch."

He scoffed and licked his bottom lip with a laugh. "Because there's no way that a woman would want to be friendly with me otherwise."

"I know you put persuasion on her!" Clara yelled and I was surprised and how hateful it sounded.

"Clara," I hissed.

"Fay, you don't know him."

"Yes, I do."

"No, you don't." This was from Enoch. He smiled evilly and self-deprecating. He came toward me and looked down at me. "The funs over, princess. Time to go back to the real world."

"Take it off, Enoch," Clara said through gritted teeth.

"Clara," I scolded. "Will you just—"

"You're under persuasion. You have no idea what you actually think or feel right now." She glared over at him before looking at me. We had a small audience gathering. I glanced over at Eli to see what kind of faith he had in his brother and it didn't appear he had amassed any in that corner either. I glared at him and rolled my eyes.

He seemed to get the message and stepped in. "CB, come on. They've had a long trip. Let them get settled in."

"After he takes the persuasion off," she seethed. "I know he put it on her." She looked at him, her eyes orbs of hate. "Didn't you?"

"Yes," Enoch answered easily.

She gasped and looked at me as if that answered everything. "See!"

"I knew that, Clara." I sighed in exasperation. "He told me all about it and explained what it was and why he put it on me."

She squinted and looked between us. "What?" She stared at me. "How…much do you know?"

"About what?" I smirked. "About devourers? About witches? About Enoch feeding on people's emotions? About the Horde chasing us? Should I go on?"

"The Horde is chasing you?" She glared at Enoch extra hard. "You suck!"

"He saved me," I reminded her. "Over and over again. They were looking for me and would have found me if not for that devourer. Right there, the one you're glaring at."

She huffed. "Take. The. Persuasion. Off."

Enoch uncrossed his arms and left his brother's side. He came my way and seemed uneasy about this, which made me uneasy about it. "What's the matter?" I whispered.

He smiled where no one could see but me.

"Are you afraid once you take off the persuasion she won't like you anymore?" Clara taunted and crossed her arms, tapping her foot angrily. "You afraid that your persuasion was the only thing keeping her around, Enoch?"

Enoch licked his lip and sighed, his breath hitting my cheek. "Yes," he said. "That's exactly what I'm afraid of."

He sounded so wounded that even Clara had the good sense not to go any further. She stayed quiet while he took my face in his hands. He swiped his thumb over my lips once and let his smile shine through just barely.

"Look in my eyes, princess."

"I hate when you call me that," I said, but I felt my smile.

"No, you don't," he whispered. "Fay, I want you to feel your mind as it's freed from my persuasion. Feel it slip and be free, knowing that your thoughts are your own, your feelings are your own. Everything that happens or has happened is real and you have to deal with it, okay? Everything's going to be all right."

"Okay," I whispered.

I felt so light. His hands on my cheeks were so warm it was ridiculous. And then things started to click. Things weren't normal. There were demons and witches and...devourers. He had fed off my fear... I looked up at him and knew that right now...this moment, how I handled this, would be the catalyst for everything to come after. I took a deep breath and tried to smile.

"Thanks for saving me. Again."

His mouth actually dropped open and he looked completely shocked. His mouth formed words several times, but nothing came out. But then Clara had to ruin it in typical Clara fashion.

"Excuse me!" she shrieked. We turned to look at her. "What the hell do you mean 'thanks for saving me again," she mocked me in a weird voice. "You don't expect me to believe that Enoch Thames put persuasion on you and didn't take advantage of you in some way."

I glared. "Yes. I'm telling you that's what happened."

"No, no, no. Look at him. He's as shocked as I am. He thought you were going to hate him, too. There has to be a reason for that—which means he thought when you came out of the persuasion you'd be angry with him for what you remembered and felt." She looked at me expectedly. "So, what do you remember?"

The first thing I did was grip Enoch's arms so he couldn't run away. I wanted him here. He had put persuasion on me, yes, but it *had been* to protect my mind. I had been angry at him when he told me but I could see that now.

"I was coming to find you," I told her, but my eyes were on him. "I didn't have enough for a hotel so I was sleeping in my car. A man…" Without Enoch's persuasion to keep me from crumpling, it all came rushing back as I told her, just as if it were happening. I felt a sob bubble up. "A man attacked me in the parking lot. He was going to…" I shook my head and felt Enoch wipe a tear from under my eye with his thumb.

"Don't, love," his voice rumbled.

I let my gaze swing over to Clara and she and Eli both were staring—gaping—at the scene Enoch and I were making. I didn't know why, but I had to keep going. I had to finish. It was like word vomit. I had to get it out.

"Enoch was passing by and he stopped the man from…hurting me. And then he got me food and a place to sleep that night."

"Yeah," Clara scoffed, "for a price, I'm sure."

"It was for a price," I agreed and Clara came forward.

"She's my sister, you bastard."

"I had to help him find someone to feed from."

She stopped, or rather Eli stopped her, wrapping his arms around her from behind. He pressed his face to hers from behind and tried to soothe her.

"Baby, just wait," he whispered in his lilting tone. But even he seemed so confused. He looked at Enoch, who had moved back from me a little, but still held my arm in his hand as if he needed to protect me at any moment. "You didn't feed from Clara's sister?"

"Fay," I corrected, annoyed, and sighed.

He smiled. "Sorry."

Enoch sighed gruffly. "I never forced any emotions out of her."

"Then who have you been feeding from?" Eli asked, puzzled and a little hysterical.

Enoch sighed even heavier this time. "Can we talk about this later." It wasn't a question. His gaze roamed around and Eli followed his eyes to the crowd gathering.

Clara pulled from Eli, turning to give him a kiss, and then glared at Enoch as she passed. She took my arm from his. "Come on, Fay. We've got a lot of catching up to do."

When I turned back to look, Enoch was one-arm hugging Eli, and Eli looked about as surprised as someone could look. He finally caught up and they patted each other on the back. "What?" Clara asked, but when she finally looked back, they had stopped hugging and she missed it.

"Nothing. So..." I looked around at the little tents and cabins everywhere. "You live in the woods."

She laughed. "Technically, you're not supposed to be here. I guess I should thank Enoch for that. If you hadn't been with him, Franz wouldn't have brought you here."

"Why?"

She looked at me as we walked. "How much do you know? Really?"

"I know that they're lots of supernatural things out there. The Horde came after us."

"About that." She turned and gave me the sorriest look. "That has to be because of me. I'm so sorry."

I nodded. "They said they wanted to use me to find you and Eli."

She gasped. "Oh, my..." She hugged me to her. "I'm *so* sorry."

"It's okay. Enoch was there and he saved my life." I leaned back and made her look me in the face. "He saved my life over and over and not because I was doing anything for him. In reality, I never actually even got him anyone to feed from. He just kept taking care of me."

She put her hand up and spoke slow, like I was a toddler. "Okay, I'm going to tell you some things, and I know it's going to be hard to hear, but I want you to listen good." I sighed, but she went on. "Enoch is evil. There isn't a good bone in his body. He doesn't do things for nothing. There is always a reason or motivation for the things he does, and if he has used you this whole time with this goody-goody act, then he's trying to get to me through you. He's going to hurt you to hurt me. You see? He knows that you're the most important person to me, the only person I have left in the whole world and so he sought you out, found you, and pulled this *I'm-cured* act to try to make you fall in love with him. Then he'll bail, break your heart, and we'll pay for it. Don't fall for it, Fannie."

My heart was breaking already. I seethed. "I hate when you call me that." I turned, but she bolted to get in front of me.

"I know. I'm sorry. Look, you don't know him like I do. Like we all did. He is the vilest man—no, creature—you've ever known!"

"You weren't with him, Clara."

"Neither were you! You were under persuasion the entire time!" I straightened my back and she knew she'd gone too far. "I'm sorry, I'm sorry. Look." She sighed and touched her forehead. "I don't know how to get through to you."

"Clara, you weren't with us. You don't know the things he did."

"What do you mean?"

"It wasn't just me he saved. He went back into a restaurant and saved an entire building full of people when I was already safe outside. He saved them from the Horde." She squinted and leaned back against a tree, looking pissed and puzzled. I leaned against it with her and started from the beginning, all the way back to the guy at the hotel who tried to rape me. And…I told her how I was discharged from the military and why. I told her everything. When I finally finished, it was almost dark and a bell started to ring. She was stunned silent.

"Dinner," she muttered and stood. "Holy wow, Fay. I can't believe you went through all that...because of me."

"I had to find you." I shuffled my feet and looked down in shame. "I've never felt so ashamed as I have for how I handled you after Mom and Dad."

She wrapped her arms around my neck. "They were your mom and dad, too. It wasn't your job to take care of me."

I scoffed and hugged her tighter. "But it was, Clara. It was. I'm so sorry I let you down."

She leaned back and I was so surprised to see her eyes full of tears. "Nah. I was happy with the pastor and Mrs. Ruth. They were really good to me. In fact, we're going to try to go back to see them for Thanksgiving. All the babies are getting so big. I'll tell them to set a plate for you if we can work it out. No buts."

"Okay," I said and wiped my eyes.

We started to follow the flow of people to a big tent in the center of everything.

"So Eli?" I asked. "He's like Enoch. A devourer, too?"

"He used to be. A witch took it from him and he's human now. Mostly," she said with a smile.

"So he doesn't have to...feed off of emotion anymore?"

"Nope. He has to eat food to survive now." We reached Eli and she poked his flat stomach as he handed each of us a plate. "And he has to watch calories like the rest of us now."

They laughed and I raised an eyebrow. Eli laughed again. "Inside joke."

"Where's Enoch? He's not eating?"

They both looked at me funny. "Enoch doesn't eat human food. Except Cheetos."

I gave them both an equally funny look. "But he ate on the trip with me all the…time."

As their strange looks drained away to even stranger ones, I realized that they were not going to be accepting of the new Enoch, not matter how hard he tried. He must have been a real doozy of a guy before.

"Okay, well even if he doesn't eat, I'm sure they're tons of people here that he hasn't seen in a long time."

Clara scoffed. "Trust me. No one here missed him."

I handed them back the plate and crossed my arms. "Where is he?"

"Fay, don't," Clara tried.

"By the river," Eli said at the same time.

I walked away without looking back. I was starving, but seriously, for them to treat him as if he weren't welcome after everything he'd done for me was just not acceptable.

It was almost dusk, and the small bit of light made his silhouette against the sky absolutely beautiful. I stared at it for a few long seconds before he noticed me and I saw his head hang. I felt that small ache in my gut—that he didn't want to see me. But I wasn't backing down now. I walked slowly toward him, crossing my arms behind my back, and tried for a small smile. "Hey."

"You should go eat something," he said roughly and looked back out at the water. The old me would have took that as what it was and left with her tail between her legs.

"Come eat with me."

He laughed, no humor in sight. "What I need I can't get from you."

I flinched. He saw. He opened his mouth, but didn't say anything.

"Okay, Enoch," I said with a pathetic sigh. "You're the type that lashes out and hurts people when they get upset. Okay. I remember."

And I did. I remembered all the things that happened, all the things he kept me from feeling on our trip, but now I remembered everything that we talked about. How I felt so drawn to him and he kept me at arm's length, not once taking advantage of me, even though Clara had said he would have.

"When someone wants to change or goes through something that makes them different…it doesn't matter what they were, it only matters what they want to be."

"It can't really be that simple to humans, can it?"

"Why not?"

"Because the rest of the world is anything but."

I closed my eyes, remembering the way his fingers had felt on my cheek, it all rushed back to me just like it was happening in that moment. My…my entire being warmed just remembering it.

I opened my eyes and saw Enoch clenching his fists. I saw when he truly registered what I was thinking about. His mouth opened slightly and his eyes took on a drugged look.

"Did you know that when you took the persuasion off," I began and moved toward him, "when I remember things that happened, it's like they're happening in real-time?" My voice sounded entirely too breathy, but I couldn't stop. "Like it's happening right now? I'm thinking about that night at the hotel—"

He cursed. "Fay, don't do this to me. I can't control myself right now. I *really* need to feed."

"So feed from me. I never understood why you didn't want to."

"No," he said vehemently and took a step back when I'd almost reached him.

"Why?" I asked. He may as well have thrown cold water on me. He licked his lip, but there was nothing left. "Ok, you had me under persuasion before. You didn't want to take advantage of me. That was noble and sweet, Enoch." He scoffed. "But I'm not anymore, and I get why you did everything you did on the trip. You still need to feed from someone. I can tell that you're already starting to get…jumpy again. What are you going to do?"

"I'll have to feed, Fay," he said and stared at me as if I was missing something.

"Why not me?" I moved until I was right in front of him, even though he tried to take a step or two back. "Why? Is it Clara? I'll handle Clara."

"No, it's not Clara," he answered, like that was ridiculous.

"So, it's just me then." I backed away and covered my mouth as I turned. To keep in a sob? To keep from saying something stupid? Who knew. "Um…thank you."

"For what?" he whispered.

For all I knew when we woke up tomorrow, he would have skipped out on us, on me, so I made myself turn and say what was on my mind. But when I looked at him, the tears came. I smiled and said it anyway. "Thank you for saving me. You didn't have to stop that night. You could have kept going and never had to put up with me and all the troubles I brought with me."

"Fay," he sighed and shook his head.

"I know the Horde was coming after me, not you. You could have been free of all this and just gotten away from it all. You came back because of me." I looked back at the group of people who were going down the line of food in the open tent. "And judging by that chilly reception you got, I can see why you would want to stay away." I swung my gaze back and he had moved right up against me. I barely gasped, but had to keep going. "Thank you for doing what you did, to keep me sane. If you hadn't persuaded me, I would have just been freaking out the whole time. You helped my mind let it settle in. No matter what Clara says, it was actually easier to accept things that way. And then you saved me again and again. And you…" I shook my head. "I wouldn't be here if not for you. I wouldn't be alive if not for you. And I never would have made it all the way here on only a few bucks anyway. I don't know what I would have done if you hadn't come along."

He just looked down at me, his eyes wide and honest. "So even after talking to Clara, and her telling you what a horrible bastard I am, you still think I'm worth saving?"

I took the end of his shirt in my fingers. "I did most of the talking," I said with a small chuckle and looked up at him from under my lashes. "I told her all about our trip, everything that happened. She said you were…" I shook my head. "It doesn't matter. I don't know that old you; I only know the you that's standing in front of me."

"Where the hell did you come from?" he muttered and looked so torn. He gulped and looked around, back toward the tent. "You should go eat something before everything's gone."

"You're not coming, I take it."

He looked away, not saying anything. I knew that when I woke up in the morning, he would be gone. I'd never see him again, but I'd be forced to remember him forever by staring at his brother's face. I reached up and put my arms around his neck. His arms went wide, his rebellion at the idea.

I laughed. "It's okay. You don't have to hug me back." I sighed into his hair and pressed myself as close as I could get up on my tiptoes. His hand splayed on the small of my back and the other hand reached up to cup my neck. "Thanks for everything, Enoch."

"Why do you sound like you're saying goodbye?"

"Because I have a funny feeling that you'll be gone by morning."

He leaned back, our faces so close. "How do you know me so well?"

I smiled. "I thought you said I didn't know you at all?"

"Fay!"

We turned toward the screech and saw Clara glaring at us from the top of the hill.

"Go," he said and took a step back, his hands falling away. "You got your sister. You made it here. You got everything you ever wanted, right? Someday you're going to find some smashing human and make beautiful babies together," he murmured almost angrily and then smiled at me. "Of that I have no doubt, love."

"So you are leaving," I confirmed and the tears fell freely. Knowing he wasn't going to be there was heartbreaking. He sucked in a breath, licking his lip as he came my way once more.

He lifted his hand slowly and with his forefinger wiped a tear from my cheek so reverently, it made me cry even harder. He gripped his chest with free hand and sighed. "Sorry. I know you hate to taste my—"

"No," he sighed, his eyes closed. When they opened, he unleashed his gaze on me. "These tears are for me. No one has ever cried for me before." I looked at him and silently begged him to stay. He leaned in and whispered, "This is a beautiful gift, Fay."

"Enoch—"

He leaned in and I held my breath, but his lips didn't connect with mine. They brushed my cheek and I was once again wondering what Enoch felt for me. "Thank you. Now go, eat."

"You need to feed."

"I do," he agreed, and he did. I could see how awful he was starting to look.

"But you don't want to feed from me."

"No, Fay," he said harder and gulped.

That solidified it for me. I'm not sure what our trip was, but it hadn't meant the same thing to him. I tried to hide it, but it still must have shown on my face before I turned.

"Fay," he sighed.

I didn't stop. I didn't want his sympathy. And that's what it was. I shook my head at myself. Ah, I was so stupid! Even just now when I was crying! He had said it was a beautiful gift. That's because he was trying to let me down easy. Because he thought I was psycho for crying in the first place! I finger combed my hair and went inside. A few nosy people tried to act like they weren't staring at me, but I just ignored them. Clara and Eli watched me like a hawk as I grabbed a bowl of spaghetti and sat with a thud on the green grass to eat it. I wasn't even hungry anymore really, but I made myself eat.

I looked over to find them watching me and sighed. I waved them over and Clara practically bounded. "Why the hell do you have cry eyes?" she hissed.

"Because I was crying."

"What did he do?"

"I was thanking him, Clara," I said, exasperated. "Can I just eat in peace and take a shower, if you have them…and maybe get some clothes. I just want to go to bed."

"Yes." She had the good sense to say that and only that, but she looked like she wanted to say a lot more.

Eli walked off to where his brother had been and I tried to put it out of my mind. There was a community shower at the campground, so that was *fun*. Clara and I were still the exact same size, so no problems there. I got some sleep clothes and some clothes for the next day. There were some tents and some cabins.

Clara and Eli had a very small camper-type thing. I shared with them and took the pull-out couch. So I crawled under the covers and pulled them over my head, trying not to think about anything. It amazed me how different my mind was now that the persuasion was off. I worried about things now that I hadn't thought about as much just a couple days ago.

I drifted to sleep, trying to forget that what was supposed to be a happy day for me, a day of reunions and love, just reminded me how much I always felt like I was the one that wasn't good enough and no one wanted around.

I felt arms under my breasts and could remember his breath as it skated over my cheek. *I'll give you a place to stay for the night. No charge. You give me a little something in return, okay?* I balled up in on myself and tried to catch my breath. Was it real? Had it all been a dream and I was still caught in the hotel guy's clutches?

"Fay?"

I pushed the hands off me and scooted away. "No!" I shouted.

"Fay," someone said softly and touched my hair. I opened my eyes and found myself looking at my sister. "Clara?"

She nodded. I looked past her to find a shirtless Eli peeking out to check on us. "Everything okay out here, baby?"

"We're okay," she said and looked back. When she saw him she got up and climbed over the bed to him quickly. She whispered something to him and then kissed him. He took her face in his hands, not letting her get away, and kissed her again softer, longer. I felt like I was prying by watching, but I couldn't look away. So this was who my sister married. You could tell he worshipped the ground she walked on, and would do anything for her. And it was mutual. She didn't abuse that, and that surprised me. I always assumed when she got married she'd be a bridezilla who ordered her husband around and I'd feel sorry for him, but I could tell that the respect was mutual. I found myself wanting to cry as I watched them.

They separated and he smiled, putting his forehead to hers for just a second. "I love you. Yell if you need anything."

"I love you," she whispered back.

"Fay, you need anything?" he asked wryly.

"No," I said and laughed. "Thank you for letting me stay."

"Of course."

Clara bit her lip as she watched him go and then crawled up on the bed beside me again. "Bad dream?"

"Yeah. Weird that I haven't had any until tonight."

"The persuasion was keeping them away," she said with a sigh.

"And that's not a bad thing," I said and lay down with a sigh of my own. I stared at the ceiling. "No offense, but I never thought you'd wind up living with a group of gypsies. In a travel trailer no less."

She busted out laughing. "Oh, me either, honey. Me either. I have so much to tell you."

She turned and hugged me around my back, her hands resting on my stomach. She began to talk and told me how Eli came into the picture, about Tate, about Enoch, Eli giving up everything—his very being—to save her life, them getting married. I told her I got the invitation, but it came too late all because I had been a coward and ran and they couldn't find me in time. She hugged me tight and said it didn't matter, that I was there now. She said we could talk more tomorrow, that I could ask anything I wanted. She would show me pictures if I wanted of the wedding. I nodded, but it wasn't really the same.

I fell asleep and had no more problems with dreams of people trying to hurt me.

———————

The smell of bacon woke me, but the sounds of giggles and deep, but quiet moans kept me from getting up. I peeked my eyes opened and saw bacon in the pan with biscuits on the stove. Clara's butt was planted firmly on the counter top, Eli thankfully had a shirt on now, but it didn't even matter because Clara was practically ripping it off the guy.

When he gripped her butt and dragged her closer to him, crushing her to him, I couldn't even be embarrassed really. I was the older sister and I had wasted my life. I had never had that with anyone. If anything, I was jealous. Happy for her, but jealous.

He groaned again with a throaty little chuckle and I knew I had to let them know I was awake. I rolled my eyes and cleared my throat. "Um, I'm awake now!" I said loudly. "Very, very awake!"

Clara just laughed and Eli sighed, pulling her from the counter and straightening their clothes. I could tell that he was the straight-laced one, the level-headed and sensible one of the two of them. "Sorry, Fay." He smiled and made a plate before handing it to me. "Breakfast?"

"Clara cooks?"

She snorted. He smiled wider. "Uh, no. We don't eat a communal breakfast so we eat in the mornings on our own. But Clara hasn't really mastered...the stove."

She laughed and poked his stomach. "That's a sweet way of saying I almost burned the camper down. Twice."

I laughed, biting into my bacon. She shook her head. "No, here, sis. Make a sandwich." She put bacon in my biscuit and put a little jelly from a jar on the counter. "One of the ladies here makes this homemade grape jelly. I'm telling you, it's amazing with Eli's biscuits and bacon."

"Sounds gross." I made a scrunched up face.

"Eat it!" she ordered with a laugh. I took a bite and was pleasantly surprised. "It's good, Eli." He smiled and shrugged. I walked over to him. "Thank you for taking care of her for me, while I was gone."

He smiled. "Of course."

"No, I mean it. You gave your life for her." He looked at her and back at me with a sigh.

"Someone was up talking late last night, huh?"

"It's what sisters do," she reasoned.

I threw my uncomfortableness out the window and hugged him around his middle. I may have hugged him a bit too hard, because I heard him *oomph* and then chuckle.

"I don't know you," I said, hearing the tears threatening. I sighed at myself for the ridiculous amount of crying I was doing lately. "But you not only saved my sister, you took care of her and obviously make her happy." I looked at Clara and knew she was happy. Like in her soul happy. "Thank you for that."

He squeezed me back. He felt so much like Enoch. "She made me happy first." I heard the smile in his voice. I knew there was probably a great story there that I wasn't privy to, but I also knew he wasn't going to tell me. "Seriously, you don't ever have to thank me for that. She saved me, too."

I laughed as I backed away and sniffed. "Those accents are freaking adorable." I wiped my nose. "Where are you and Enoch from?" Just saying his name made my chest hurt knowing that I was never going to see him again.

"A little bit of everywhere." His eyes shifted to the window. "Why don't you ask him?"

My heart begged him not to be playing with me as I turned to find Enoch coming toward the trailer. I stood frozen in my spot. He hadn't left. He was walking awfully fast. And that guy...Franz something-or-other was with him. They knocked once and then opened the door without waiting.

"Eli!" Franz bellowed and then stepped inside.

Enoch came in next and stopped dead in his tracks when he laid eyes on me. I gulped. He slowly closed the door.

"Fay," he said in a whispered hello. "Nice pajamas." He let his eyes take me in starting with my feet, and just like last time he wasn't shy about letting me see that he was very much enjoying the view.

"Stop eye-raping my sister and get on with whatever you barged in here for," Clara barked.

"Clara!" I snapped. "I am a grown woman. I can tell someone to stop looking at me if I want him to. Which I clearly don't or I would have told him to stop." I sighed at the level of awkwardness. "Now we can get on with the business." I sat and looked at the Franz guy and waited patiently.

He smirked and laughed just once at Clara before getting serious. "Ok then. Uh…I hate to say this, Fay. It's not your fault, so don't feel bad, but the Horde followed you here."

I stood. "No."

"It's all right. We've fought them before. We fight them a lot. They held back and made you both think you were clear of them so you'd lead them to us."

"And we did." I walked to the window, leaning on the counter. "That ambush at the restaurant…that was probably just a trap. If we had left like you asked, Enoch, we probably would have gotten away, but you went back to save those people because I asked you to and now…"

"Saved people," Clara whispered, but I shook my head.

"It doesn't matter," I muttered.

I felt a hand on my shoulder and turned to find Enoch, but expected Clara. He pulled his hand away.

"You're still here," I whispered. "I thought you were going to leave at first light."

He looked at my lips and then my eyes. "I thought I was, too. But when it came time to leave, I just…didn't want to go. And then Franz told me that a small group of the Horde was surrounding the bank on the other side."

"Ah," I said, understanding. "You *couldn't* leave."

"There's not that many of them, Fay. I can leave if I want to," he said harder. I stared up at him, wishing I didn't want him to want me. I licked my lip and his eyes jumped to watch the movement. When he blinked, it was sluggish and slow. I was so confused. He seemed to be angry all of a sudden. He glared at me and leaned back on the counter, pushing the breath from his lips in a huff. "Can we talk about what we came here to talk about now?" he barked.

I turned to look out the window and just begged myself not to cry. It worked. I tried to listen to them as they talked about an ambush and then packing up and leaving, moving somewhere else in the dead of night before their reinforcements showed up.

"They don't know that we know they're here, so we have the upper hand," Franz was saying. "We need to move fast or we'll lose it."

"Enoch, you need to feed. We all need to be at our strongest."

"I know that," he growled. "I searched all night, but there was nothing. People in the rebel camp don't fight, believe it or not. So I'm…going to have to think of something else."

"Well," Eli said carefully, "we have other Devourers in the camp. "There are people here that cater to their needs, to feed them. I'm sure someone would be willing to do the same for you."

I snapped my gaze over to them and knew exactly what they were talking about. Enoch didn't look at me, not at all. He nodded once and barged out the door with Franz on his tail. Franz yelled for us to meet everyone else in thirty minutes.

I went straight to the bathroom, grabbing the clothes Clara had given me to get dressed first. But all I could think about was Enoch getting fed from someone that wasn't me. And then I remembered what he told me last night.

But you don't want to feed from me?

No, Fay.

He had told me flat out that he didn't want to feed from me. And just now, he told me flat out that the only reason he hadn't left was because the Horde was blocking his way. And now he was going to feed from some other girl. I didn't know why he had such a strong connection and hold on me, but I had to let this go. Yes, he saved me; yes, I thought he was…more, but he made it clear that for him, I wasn't.

So I got dressed and used Clara's stuff in the bathroom to fix my hair and threw on a little bit of her makeup. I waited for Clara and Eli and then we met the rest of the rebels in the big tent for the meeting to discuss a plan of action. I didn't let my eyes roam around, though I knew right where he was. He stood on the other side of Eli, not too far from us. And he kept looking back at me. It pissed me off, too. Why would he look back, why did he care?

They talked about sending a couple of people over the long way around the river bank and catching them on the back side to ambush them. We'd be leaving in the early, early morning. When they dismissed the group, I was the first one to bolt from the tent. It was probably good that we were leaving. He would leave, too, and—

"Fay." His warm, strong grip took my arm and turned me, not giving me the choice.

My mouth fell open and I glared at his hand. "What?" I snapped.

He clenched his jaw, his fingers tightened. "I want you to stay clear of this. Just stay in the trailer, even if Clara gets it in her head to get involved. Don't."

I laughed and shook my head. "I'm not the hero type. That's your job."

"I'm not a hero."

"Yes, you are," I hissed and gulped. "You are a hero. You save people, over and over, and then when you finally bring them home, you completely derail and act like a jackass who doesn't know how to handle it." I yanked my arm away.

He gave an angry chuckle. "Jackass, huh?"

"You are the not the same person who was on that trip with me." I leaned forward a little. "You want to leave and be in the next stolen car out of here like a coward, then fine. Because you're not him anyway. I miss that guy. I miss the guy who helped me and made sure I ate enough and got enough sleep and put my feet in his lap when he thought I wouldn't know about it." He looked angry, but I kept going. "The guy who went into a building and saved complete strangers for me. The guy who got angry and told me not to…make him fall for me, and we never spoke of it again." He gulped, looking so vulnerable. My no-crying rule went out the window and a sob caught in my throat. "I miss him and you're not him! As soon as we got here, he was taken from me."

I turned to leave but heard a loud bang. I stopped, but was yanked roughly, and before I knew what was happening, Enoch's pained face was right in front of mine and all the puzzle pieces were coming together. I searched for the wound and found it easily in his chest. "No! Enoch!"

We stumbled to the ground on our knees. He groaned and used his fist to keep himself upright.

"Help!" I screamed. "Help!"

But then I was on my back under him on the ground and he was shielding me once again, looking around for more trouble, a horrible pained but determined look on his handsome face.

"Enoch, what are you doing?" He sighed and relaxed, giving me the indication that there was no longer any danger. He relaxed his weight on me before rolling off into the grass on his back, his face drawn and his breaths labored. I sat up and leaned over him, still low to the ground. "Oh, God, Enoch."

"It's okay," he said. I shook my head and put my hand on his chest. "Fay, I'm all right," he insisted.

"You've been shot," I sobbed. "Oh, my God, no. It's in your heart." I cried harder. "No. You jumped in front of me. You took this bullet for me." I looked at his face, so mad at him. "Why are you always being the hero!"

He chuckled and winced. "I'm not human, Fay. I'll be fine."

"That doesn't mean it's okay for you to get shot for me!"

He tried to smile. I could tell he was enjoying this. "Sweetheart—"

"Don't *sweetheart* me," I scolded and sniffed. "You do these things and then blow me off, be a complete ass to me, and I…" He was looking at me guiltily, like he knew it was true. I sighed. "I guess I could scold you when you don't have a bullet in your chest."

The edges of his lips lifted. "I am an ass. We'll…talk, okay? But this?" He pointed to his chest and the bullet hole. "I'll be fine. You can't kill a devourer like this. You can even break our necks and we won't die. I'll be fine. I saw the bullet coming and I had to stop it."

"Speaking of," I looked over his chest across the river, "who's trying to shoot me?"

He stuck his finger in his chest and dug the bullet out. I hissed as he flicked it to the ground and watched him stand. He held his hand out for me and glared across the river as he pulled me up. He shielded me the entire time as he blurred me along the bank until we were hidden behind a large tree.

"Stay at the camp. Go to the trailer like I told you." He looked at me. "I mean it, Fay. I can't be hurt, I'll be fine, but you can. I don't want to have to worry about you."

He'd never sounded so sincere, or looked it either. My hand was still wrapped in his from where he helped me up from the ground. I looked down at entwined hands, thinking he'd pull away, but he didn't. He squeezed my fingers and lifted my chin. "Fay," he growled in a whisper. "Don't make me worry about you."

"I'll stay. You're not going over there by yourself, are you?"

"Eli's human now. He's useless," he sneered and then remembered that I was one, too. He looked at me. "Sorry. But when it comes to fighting our kind, a human wouldn't stand a chance."

"I don't disagree with you."

"I'm going to find Franz." We looked around the grounds at people who were bustling about, trying to find the culprit, to see if anyone else has been hit. But there had only been one shot— one shot and it had been aimed at me.

I gripped his fingers tighter. "Those people are looking all around for more shots, but there had only been one. And it was meant for me."

"Right now I need to bust their heads for trying it," he said harshly. He paused, waited, stalled—something—as he looked at me. He took the small step to close the gap between us. "When I heard that shot and imagined what would happen if you had taken that bullet instead of me..."

I let my confusion show. "Enoch," I shook my head, "you hate me." I laughed my words to keep from crying.

"I thought we talked about this," he said quietly, a small private smile on his lips, "and we said that hating you wasn't possible."

"But the way you act goes a lot farther than the things you say."

He nodded and gulped. I noticed that he did that so much. "I can't be what you want me to be," he whispered, anguished.

"I don't want you to be anything but what you are."

He was back to looking angry. "What I am is a bastard. I am a bad guy who does bad things. You deserve a lot more than that."

"Can't you just avenge me now and we'll talk about it later," I said coyly. I smirked and hoped he took the bait. He laughed reluctantly and looked pained.

He rubbed his face, my hand still in his and he leaned forward. He kissed my forehead and once again I was aching for those lips to head south. "You are killing me..."

"Little human," I finished and smiled. "I know."

"And yet you still do it," he muttered and smiled. "You seem to be enjoying it."

"Oh, I am."

He chuckled before grabbing a passing man's shirt collar. "Take Fay to Eli's place. Make sure she's safe inside before you leave. Got it?"

The guy nodded without question. "Of course."

Enoch sighed as he walked backward from me, watching me like a predator watches his prey.

"I'll be back," he promised, but it wasn't a sweet gesture, it was more like a warning. "Be ready."

"I'm ready," I said. "Be careful."

He grinned and pointed at himself. "Not human, princess. I'll be fine."

He turned to sprint, but turned once more and gave me a stern look, his chin dropping down. "I better find you at the trailer with Eli and Clara, or you will be in so much trouble."

I smiled, unable to help myself. "That doesn't sound so bad."

He groaned and put his fist to his mouth. I laughed and held my hand up. "Okay. I'm going."

I couldn't help but feel like a million pound weight had been lifted off my chest as we walked through the trees, to give us cover, the guy said. He also said if anything happened to me that Enoch would rip his head off. I looked up at him and couldn't stop my intake of breath. He wasn't human—that was obvious given by the fact that the irises of his eyes weren't just white and almost clear, but swirling and alive. I tried my cover my discomfort and show him that I was...fine, I was just still adjusting. "What's your name?"

"Aries." His voice was gruff.

"Like the God of war?"

He smiled and looked over at me. "Smart girl. It's not spelled the same, but I like to think that I can hold my own in a fight."

"You don't have many humans here, do you?" I asked softly.

"No, not many." He stopped walking and turned to face me. "We don't have any that aren't mated or bound to someone. That's their reason for being here."

"Bound?" I asked and stepped closer.

He smiled and the affection oozed from him as he lifted his arm. You can't see it because you're a human, but there's a string on my wrist attaching me and my mate together."

I grimaced. "Really?"

He laughed. "Yeah. I thought girls were supposed to eat that romantic stuff up?"

"It's essentially a leash?" He laughed harder. "So she can't get away, right?"

"No way." He bent over a little, laughing, before giving me a look that said he thought I was adorable. I frowned at that. "Wow, you're a tough cookie." He paused, looking me over. "No. It means she chose me. Our kinds— devourers, witches, goblins," he pointed to himself, "necromancers. We find someone that we want to spend some time with, and no one else, and they are our mate. It can last for a long time or a short time, but they are ours and no one else's. But when the bond goes deeper than that, more than just lust and wanting, when it becomes…love, a bond can take place." He held up his wrist again. "It looks like a vine wrapped around my wrist, kind of like smoke, and it flows all the way to my mate. I can find her anywhere and her, me. So she can never be taken from me or be lost. I'll always be able to keep her safe even if I'm not right beside her."

I thought about that. "That *is* kind of romantic.

He chuckled and bumped my arm with his elbow. "Now you're getting it." He beckoned me along. "Come on. If I don't get you inside soon, Enoch will murder me."

"You know him?"

He scoffed. "Yes, I know him, but even if I didn't, everyone knows who he is. The Thames brothers are devourer royalty." I snapped my gaze over and he laughed. "I didn't figure he was going to spill the beans about that."

"But you are, aren't you?" I coaxed and smiled sweetly.

He laughed loudly, his head leaned back. "Wow, you a mess, little human."

I sulked. "Why does everyone call me that?"

He finished his laugh and then nodded. "Yeah, I'll tell you. Because I like your spunk and I know that you want to know for the right reasons."

"And what reasons are those?" I asked as I pulled a small twig from a bush to busy my hands.

The corners of his lips lifted. "Enoch is different than he used to be. The Thames family is the kingship family of the devourers. They rule, so to speak. They were rich, they were powerful, they were mean, and they were cunning." I squinted, thinking of Eli. He didn't strike me as that way at all. Neither did Enoch, but Eli didn't especially. Hundreds of years ago…" He waited to see if I was going to compute that. I nodded for him to go on. "They ruled everything. Devourers are kind of the big dogs of everybody. Eli was set to take over everything. And then he just disappeared. No one sees him for years. Come to find out he had some kind of existential breakdown. It changed him. A little boy made him view things differently and he didn't want to feed anymore. So he stopped forcing emotions on people and only fed when people were—"

"Yeah, I know."

He nodded. "So. Enoch finds him later, after he'd met Clara. But by that time the Horde had gotten out of control. Enoch couldn't take over the family. His family was destroyed, the entire structure of the system we'd always known was crumbling because of a few idiots who didn't want to let us be. Enoch always wanted to be the son to take over the family business, so to speak. When Eli didn't want it, it made him even angrier. Enoch was the more ruthless of the two back then."

"I've heard."

"But he's…not even the same person."

I laughed once. "Yeah," I whispered.

"I don't know what you did to him—"

"It wasn't me. This is the only way I've ever known him. He saved my life. That's how we met."

He smiled. "That's a good way to meet." He opened the door to Eli and Clara's trailer without knocking and paused. "People change. I hope you won't hold the person he was against him."

I looked at Clara's white tile and licked my bottom lip. "So everybody knows who Enoch was?"

"Yeah."

"But *you're* not holding that against him." I looked at him and he looked back. "You don't think this is an act on his part." I didn't phrase either of those as a question because they weren't. I looked into his eyes, making sure he knew that I wasn't afraid of their swirling or him. He seemed surprised that I was so easy with him.

He shook his head. "No. He's not acting. I've known Enoch for over a hundred years." I couldn't stop the wince. He chuckled. "Yeah. Long time. You can't fake who you are all day, all night forever. But even if he could, what would he gain from it?"

"I don't think he is. But I've only known the man he is now, not the man he used to be."

He smiled. "You said 'man'."

I frowned and sat down on the step. "What should I have said?"

"You said 'man' not 'devourer'." He smiled wider. "I'm sure Enoch would appreciate that."

I shook my head. "I doubt that. He doesn't even like humans."

"He likes you," he countered and smirked.

"Don't tell him we talked about this," I rushed to say.

"I would never," he said, fake insulted. He shooed me inside. "Inside before I get decapitated by your boyfriend."

"He's not my boyfriend."

"Yet. Stay inside and lock the door." He smiled as he walked away and turned back once more after a few steps. "I'm glad we had this talk, Fay!"

"You're worse than a woman, Aries!"

I could hear his laughter carry back to me and I found myself chuckling as I locked the door and waited for Eli and Clara to return.

What I hadn't expected was the cloth over my face, the weird smell, and the blackness that overtook me.

Eight
Enoch

"It was meant for Fay," I told them when I entered the community center. They were already talking about something, but it wasn't important. They didn't have all the facts. They were just speculating. "The shot. I took it instead and—"

"What?" I looked up from my perch on the back wall. Clara and Eli were there. She was staring at the blood on my shirt. I cursed. That meant that Fay was at the trailer alone.

"She left. I thought she was home when everything happened," Clara said in hysterics.

I paused for just a moment…and then took off out the door, blurring across the expanse of the campground until I passed Aries. I yanked him to a stop. "Hey, Enoch. You gotta stop doing that," he growled.

"Where's Fay?" I barked.

"At Eli's," he said in exasperation. "Where you asked me to take her."

"Was anyone there when you dropped her off?"

He squinted. "Not that I know of? Why?"

I took off again, but he followed me. He was fast, but not quite as fast as I was. I got there and the door was closed. I took that as I good sign. I opened the door and yelled, knowing she was going to be angry with me for scaring her, but I was scared so she could join the party. "Fay!"

No one answered. I went to the back near the bathroom. "Sweetheart, if you're in there, don't be a girl right now. Answer me." I yanked the door open so hard that one of the hinges came off. My muscles began to shake. "No. No," I begged. I sent her here. I *told* her to come here.

"Enoch," he hissed. I ran to Aries and if he showed me blood, I was going to lose it. "Look," he said and pointed out the window and we could see a clear path in the bushes in the moonlight.

I crept out the backdoor and he followed. I could hear people, Eli and Clara I imagined, running to catch up, but they would never make it in time. We followed the path silently. It clearly wasn't a devourer they had sent to take Fay. He was being far too slow, too sloppy, and too loud.

I was getting weak and needed to feed, but I had to do this. We eased along until I saw him. And when I did, I saw red. He had her thrown over his shoulder none too gently, jostling her about like a ragdoll as he trudged along. He was breathing heavy from being so out of shape that he was about to take a rest, but I blurred ahead. He turned just in time, dropping Fay in front of him. A goblin's tooth raised over Fay's neck was the only thing that stopped me from ripping his throat out. She was awake now and watching me with scared eyes. She didn't appear to be hurt, but I sucked in a breath as her fear hit me. She mouthed a 'Sorry' and I shook my head at her. She was insane if she thought I thought this was her fault.

He laughed. "Enoch Thames, in the flesh."

And then I realized something. He wasn't holding the goblin's tooth to her throat, he was holding it out towards me. Of course. I scoffed under my breath. He wouldn't think I'd have any attachment toward a human girl. But the goblin's tooth would be deadly to me—it's the only thing in the world that can kill me. He thought if he kept the tooth up towards me, I wouldn't try to take the girl. That it wouldn't be worth it to me.

"Yep." I raised my hands. "In the flesh."

"You don't stand a chance, you know that, right? I can't believe you're here, anyway. Just because your brother went soft doesn't mean you had to."

I snorted. "I'm just visiting," I said snidely. "What's it to you, troll?"

Fay tried to keep it together, but I felt her spike in fear and tightened my fist to keep from groaning. Somehow, I managed to keep it to myself. She slowly turned to look at him, her entire body shaking. I was kicking myself for saying what I'd said. He grinned at her and brought her a little closer to his face. He licked her jaw and she shuddered.

"Keep your filthy—"

"She was promised to me," he hissed, letting his long tongue snake out. "They sent me to take her and my payment for doing so was that I got to keep her." I couldn't have stopped the small step forward if I wanted to. Aries gripped my arm and the troll chuckled. "And she'll be tasty, too."

She jerked her gaze over to me and I knew that if I let him see how much she meant to me, he'd use it. He'd kill her just to spite me and he'd do it even faster. I couldn't let that happen. So even though I knew she'd be angry with me, I had to do this. "You think I care about this human?" I scoffed and it hurt every molecule in my body to do so. Her eyes searched my face, but he couldn't see her. He only watched me. "She has something on her that I need. I don't care what you do with her afterwards. I don't give a damn about a human, and the fact that you thought I did shows you don't know my reputation as well as you claim to," I growled and glared him down.

He seemed rattled, and his eyes searched the woods behind me. "Your brother and his bride—"

"Will be pissed, naturally. That's his wife's sister. But that's not my concern. I don't plan to stay here. I only came to get what I need and then I'm out of here."

"Human relations with our kinds are abominations," he spit and looked behind me to Aries. Or to the bond wrapped around his wrist rather. "They all have to be wiped out. We can't sit back while you all mix us with this trash!" he yelled in Fay's ear. She squeaked and closed her eyes, but stayed relatively still and quiet. I knew her training was to thank for that. I could imagine Clara in this scenario and the hysterics that would be abounding.

"I agree. I hate that my brother married that human."

Fay looked at me and I felt so guilty for saying it. I looked away from her.

"Well," he said and laughed a little, "this is not how I expected this night to go. I fully expected to have to kill you."

I grinned. "The night's still young."

When he leaned his head back to laugh, I roared and clapped my hands as loud as I could. Trolls are jumpy about noise, so when he winced and closed his eyes, I blurred forward. Trolls are fast, but not as fast as devourers. I knew it was going to be close. I had the jump on him, I had the advantage, and I had the upper hand because he'd thought I was on his side, but I knew he'd get the picture before we were free. I snapped his arm back away from Fay's neck and yanked her forward before slamming my fist into his chest. He swung the goblin's tooth on his way down and I felt it connect as I spun around and fell to shield Fay from anything else. Aries struck and I didn't watch.

I heard his gurgle. "This isn't over, devourer." I glared over my shoulder. "This war is far from over." I looked away as Aries ripped his throat out, and though I wanted that honor, I was happy just to have Fay safe in my arms.

I looked down at Fay under me, fully expecting her to be angry with me, but she took my face in between her cool hands and the look on her face was melting my heart. "You came for me," she said.

"Of course I did," I growled.

Aries got up and wiped the blood from his hands on his pants. "You could have been killed," he barked.

"I know that," I answered and continued to look at Fay. I wanted to remember that look on her face for the rest of my life.

"You should have let me do it. I can survive a stab from a goblin. You can't!" he yelled.

"What's he talking about? I thought you told me you couldn't be killed?" she asked and the look went away. I wanted to punch Aries for taking that look away from me.

"Aries is being dramatic. Don't worry about it." I got up and took her hands to help her stand. She fingered the slash in my shirt and eyed me wearily.

"What's this?"

Aries pushed her out of the way and I growled at him. He didn't seem to care as he stared at the hole. His eyes lifted. "You came that close to final death." His voice was quiet as he pointed at my shirt, his eyes pained.

Fay's breathing was getting heavier. "What's going on?"

He looked at her. "A goblin's tooth is the only thing that can kill a devourer. The only thing in the entire world. And that's what that troll had pointed at Enoch to keep him from getting to you."

She covered her mouth. I lifted my hand. "I'm fine. I wasn't going to just let him eat you because he *might* try to stab me."

"Eat me?"

"Trolls eat people," Aries explained, but he was looking at me. "They told him if he took you that he could eat you. And they hate noise, so that's how Enoch distracted him. But they're quick." He stepped forward. "You should have let me take him down. I can survive a stab."

"And just how were we going to discuss this plan of ours, Aries?" I said, my exasperation evident.

He sighed. "It seems like a big risk, hundreds of years of your life…" He looked back. "I'm sorry. I didn't mean it like that."

"I understand," she said. And you could tell on her face that she got it—he thought my life was worth more than hers.

I grabbed his collar lightly. "It was worth the risk. She was in that house because I sent her there." I shook my head and let him go. "Go, Aries. Thank you for your help, but I think Fay is pretty shaken up. I'm going to take her home."

He nodded and went to her. He hugged her and I felt my fists tighten. They whispered to each other and I watched. When he left, I thought I was going to spend a long time coaxing her to forgive me for the way I spoke to the troll about her, but she came right to me and threw her arms around my neck.

I sighed and lifted her feet from the ground, my arms around her tightly. She smelled divine and I couldn't stop myself as I stuck my nose into her hair and breathed deeply. She cupped the back of my head and let her fingers scratch my scalp, almost as if she was soothing me instead of the other way around. I moaned and hugged her tighter at how good it felt, how good *she* felt.

My entire universe was shifting. A human had changed me. If you had told me that a year ago, I would have broken your neck where you stood. And now, I was bloody in love with one.

"Did he hurt you?"

"My head hurts a little. I'm fine."

"Fay, I'm sorry. I didn't mean anything I said—"

"I know." She slid down my body to the ground and a little growl slipped out, but I pretended it hadn't.

"You know?" I asked, annoyed. How was she always so calm about everything? She was the least hysterical female I'd ever been in contact with.

"You just told him that so you could throw him off." Her breathing was changing. She gulped. Her eyes met mine, but then drifted down to the slash in my shirt. She looked immediately distressed. "You shouldn't have done this. Not if it meant you could die, like forever."

I chuckled under my breath. "That's usually what dying means, princess."

"Don't make fun of me, not right now." A tear finally escaped the side of her eye, just one, but it was enough to break me.

I swiped it away and pressed my lips to her forehead—just pressed them there. "I'm sorry, princess. When I knew that I'd sent you to the one place that I shouldn't have, to the place where he was going to take you from…"

"You didn't know," she argued.

"I should have made sure. I should have checked myself. I should have kept you with me."

She lifted her head and her lips quirked. "That sounds like the job of a mate."

My mouth dropped open. "What the hell did you and Aries talk about?"

She laughed softly. "Nothing, really."

"It doesn't sound like nothing."

"I wanted to know who you were." She looked up and leaned back. I knew an invitation when I saw one and she was practically yelling it. "I wanted to know who the old you was since everybody seems to think they know exactly who you are, so I asked."

I held my breath and leaned in just a bit, letting one arm snake around the small of her back. "And?"

She smiled. "And I still just know the you that I know. I don't know the person that was around a hundred years ago. If that person doesn't want to be that person anymore, then he doesn't have to be."

When she breathed out, I could feel it on my lips she was so close. It made me ache. "Why did you have to be so bloody beautiful, Fay?" She inhaled sharply. "Why did you have to have such a beautiful heart?"

Her skin practically sizzled mine as our foreheads pressed together, and I was done fighting. She gripped my collar and I slid my free hand to her ribs around to her back.

"What the hell is going on?"

Fay sighed into my mouth, and that was close to a kiss as we got. I opened my eyes to find Fay's opened, too. I loosened my grip, but I didn't let her go. Aries was with Clara and Eli, along with Franz, who seemed entirely too pleased as he grinned at me. I refused to meet his gaze.

Aries went first. "I met them on the path, told them what happened, and that you'd be bringing Fay back in a moment, but Clara wouldn't wait."

"And it's a good thing I didn't!" she yelled and gave me a look that could have killed a weaker man on the spot. "Look at him, trying to take advantage of my sister after what she just went through. I get that you need to feed and it's hard not to force emotions on people in the camp, but after what she just went through—"

"I wasn't feeding from her," I said. "I hate what her fear tastes like." She seemed taken aback and I felt Fay's hand on my chest. I hadn't realized that I'd growled it at her until I saw Eli's hand wrap around Clara's wrist. I took a deep breath. "I'm not going to hurt you, Clara. Just the thought that I want to force fear on Fay is…it's ridiculous." I shook my head, but I knew it was pointless. Clara would always see me as a monster. It would only be a matter of time before she turned Fay against me, too.

"Then what was going on?" Clara asked, quieter this time.

When Fay said nothing, I shook my head. "I'm…going to bed."

"Enoch," Fay whispered, but that one tiny noise glued me to my spot. "Stay. Please." I looked over. "Will you stay with me?"

"Fay?" Clara hissed, but I ignored her.

"Why?" I asked. I had to know why, when she knew that her sister hated me, she still wanted me to stay.

She looked at Clara. "He saved my life tonight. Again. He was the one who found out that I had been taken from your house, he followed me through the woods," she fingered the hole in my shirt, "to save me from the troll who took me."

Clara gasped and ran to her. She hugged her and cried, "Oh, my gosh, Fannie. I'm so sorry."

Fay sighed. "I hate when you call me that."

Clara winced. "Sorry. I can never remember. I'm sorry. I know that this is all a lot to take in. It's…" She shrugged. "I wish there something I could say to make it better. It seems like ever since you found out about me and Eli, you've had a rough time."

Fay looked at me. "I'm going to bed."

"That's a good idea," Clara said and took her arm.

Her eyes stayed on me. "Enoch, stay with me."

"Um…" Clara said and looked between them. "Hell no."

"On our trip to find you, Enoch kept me safe. I've never felt so safe as when I'm with him." She left Clara and looked up at me. "It's not your decision, Clara, it's Enoch's. If he doesn't want to stay with me, then—"

I took her hand and we started walking through Eli and Franz. One was smiling and one was not. I'm sure you can guess which was which. I could practically hear Clara's head exploding behind me, but I didn't care. And I wanted us to have a little time before they got there, so I turned to Fay and smiled as I put my arms around her. She looked pleasantly surprised at my pit stop and the show of affection. "Hold on tight," I whispered.

I blurred us through the trees, down the trail, all the way to Eli's. When we stopped, I fully expected to taste her fear, but her head fell back as she laughed.

"Wow," she whispered and stood up straight. "That's amazing."

"Come on," I beckoned and tugged her inside. "You may feel fine, but you still had a bad day. You need to rest."

"Thanks for staying," she said shyly as she kicked her shoes off and pulled the couch out.

"Why wouldn't I?"

"I'm sure sitting here watching me sleep isn't the most fun thing you can be doing."

I shook my head and settled into the left side of the bed. "I told you I like to sleep. I like to lie in the bed. Resting, relaxing. If

I can do that and know that you're safe, especially after the day and night that you've had?" I shook my head. "Come here."

She shook her head. "I sleep on the left side."

I laughed. "No, I sleep on the left side."

She smiled and it was gorgeous. "You. Can't. Sleep."

"Touché. I *rest* on the left side."

"Are you serious right now?" She raised her eyebrow and tilted her head. Then she bit into her lip.

I rolled my eyes and scooted over a bit, but not much. "I can't believe I was brought down by your teeth and that lip."

She giggled as she climbed in and I was hit with how normal this was. How *human*. This was what a normal couple would do. This was what Eli and Clara did, I was sure.

"What's wrong?"

I turned to find her looking at me. I shook my head. "Nothing."

"You're a really bad liar. You would think hundreds of years of living would have honed your skills."

I forced a laugh, feeling the weakness from not feeding seeping into me. "So, tell me something."

"Like what?"

I shrugged, though she couldn't see it. "Anything."

She exhaled a shaky breath. "I was dishonorably discharged from the military." I looked down at her, surprised. She went on. "I was doing everything in my power to get into trouble it seemed." She shook her head and laughed angrily. "I was so pathetic. I thought the world owed me or something. I hated being in the military, I hated that I was so far away from Clara, I hated myself, I hated that my parents were gone. I got *letters of reprimand* all the time, but the final straw was a…DUI on the base." She licked her lip a few times. I could see it in her profile. "The judge practically said I was a spoiled lost cause and stamped my final ticket home."

"He was wrong," I practically barked.

She laughed softly and reached up to rub my arm with her cool fingers. "Thanks for that, but it's okay. I deserved it. I was being stupid. If I had hurt someone…" She exhaled and I got a spike of sadness from her. She was honestly fearful about it.

"Well, I can alter my appearance," I blurted. She cocked her eyebrow. It was bloody cute. "Yeah," I reiterated. "If you saw my parents, they've altered their appearance to make themselves appear older."

"So you can look like someone else?"

"No, we can't change what we look like." She squinted, confused. "What I mean is, we can decide our age basically. Most devourers keep their age relatively young. Why wouldn't you? We stop aging at around nineteen, but if we choose it, we can alter our appearance to appear older if we like."

"Why would someone want to look old?" she asked with a little smile.

I shrugged. "My parents do it to make themselves look wiser, more respected, I guess. Less like young people and more like people we should look up to."

"More like parents?" she guessed.

I scoffed. "They were anything but good parents." She pressed her lips together in sympathy. I shook my head. "Don't feel badly for me. We don't view family the way humans do. They raised me and their job was done. I wasn't their prodigal son, the chosen one, so I...wasn't the one they focused their time on."

"That sounds awful."

I waved it away. "Tell me about your parents," I said slowly.

I expected sadness, but she smiled which surprised me greatly. Humans were such a conundrum. How was something that brought such sadness on every occasion now bringing a smile?

"They were amazing. My father would melt, literally melt, under Clara's smile." She laughed a little. "We were the biggest daddy's girls. He gave us everything we ever wanted. And my mom..." Her lip quivered. "She was the best. She gave the best advice, took us shopping, made pancakes every Saturday morning, she loved my dad like parents are supposed to love each other." She wiped under her eye as discreetly as she could. "I miss them and honestly I miss thinking about them that way. I only think about them in the ways that I miss them and they were taken from me and not in the ways that they were good to us. So thank you for that. I should do that more often."

I rubbed her head a little harder in acknowledgment. "Thanks for the history lesson. I like knowing what makes you tick."

She smiled small. "You owe me a story."

I felt a warmth settle in me as I imagined taking her in a reverie. "I've got something even better for later. Go to sleep, princess."

"What do you do while the rest of us sleep?"

"Just think," I whispered. I pulled her over to rest her head on my lap and loved the smile that spread over her face.

"Don't think too much, Enoch." I laughed a little at that and rested my head back against the headboard as I ran my hand through her hair. I knew it would help her go to sleep, and it did. In no time her breathing was slow and she was making those little noises that I was so in love with.

Bloody hell. I was goner.

Clara and Eli came in not too long after that. Clara was so mad that she almost stomped right past without even seeing us, but when she did, she boiled over.

She laid into me, in a whisper of course. "How could you do this? What is wrong with you? Why are you leading her on when you know that you're not going to act on it more than just banging her a couple times before you skip town?"

"Clara," Eli scolded and sat on the chair with a thud. He looked as drained as I felt.

"No, Eli. You know just like I do that this isn't going anywhere. It's not fair for him to let her think that there's something there when we all know there's not." She looked right at me. "She may not know you like we do, and boy do you really have her fooled, but it's cruel. I don't know why you're doing it except to hurt me, to get back at me for taking Eli from you." A sob caught in her throat and I finally saw that she wasn't just being a girl about this; she truly, honestly was worried about her sister. And I had been nothing but a monster before to her, a bastard and a monster. I deserved every bit of what she was dishing out. "I'm sorry, Enoch. I'm really sorry. But please don't take it out on her because of it. Please. She dated a lot but she's never really had a real boyfriend and…please don't do this."

Her upset and worry hit me like a sledgehammer. I sucked in a breath as quietly as I could. When I looked again, Eli had Clara in his arms and was giving me a look for upsetting his wife.

I would always be the bad guy. That was apparent.

"Eli, that little boy who made you start feeling things differently?"

He raised an eyebrow. "Yeah?"

"What happened? What did it feel like?"

"What?" Clara asked. "Why are you asking him that?"

"Because…I haven't forced an emotion to feed in over a month."

Eli immediately lit up, a smile and eyes that were hopeful. Clara, on the other hand, shook her head viciously. "No! You don't actually believe this, do you? Babe, no."

"But he hasn't been feeding," Eli reasoned. "He was starving when he showed up and has been ever since."

"That's because there's no force-feeding in the camp and he doesn't want to get kicked out."

"CB," he soothed softly and cupped her face, "look. Can we open our eyes about this? We can't have an explanation about everything, okay?"

"Yes, we can!" She pushed his hands off. "I can't believe you're picking your brother over my sister."

"That's not what's happening." He sighed. "And besides, even if it was, listen to yourself, baby."

She thought and sighed harshly. "Fine. I see your point. I don't expect you to pick my sister over your brother, but he is up to no good and I don't believe this whole *I'm changed* routine for one minute. He's just trying to get back at me for bonding myself to you."

"Fine, Clara." He sighed and rubbed his head.

I drew little circles on Fay's forehead with my thumb and enjoyed her skin, knowing this was going to have to be our last night together. Fay was fighting with her sister after just finding her, Clara and Eli were fighting, and it was all because of me. There wasn't a way to prove that I was changed. There just wasn't. Clara would never believe it and I couldn't just break up all these other relationships because I selfishly wanted one of my own.

Clara and Eli went to bed and all night I sat there and relished my time with Fay, knowing it would be short and final.

She would hate me tomorrow. I would make sure of that. It would help her get over it. I, on the other hand, would live with this in my gut forever. But it was a pain I would cherish.

The next morning, I left before anyone woke. I was getting fidgety from not feeding. Today, I'd have to feed. No way around it. And Fay wasn't going to be happy about how I had to do it. I stole a kiss from her cheek and regretted not getting to know what her lips truly tasted like. I left as silently as I could.

When I stepped from the trailer, I saw Aries and Franz talking to a witch by the river. As soon as Aries saw me, he waved and told them goodbye. He ran over in a sprint and I walked over to meet him halfway. When I reached him, I slammed him against the tree by his neck. "How dare you tell Fay all of my business?"

He smiled and patted my shoulder. "You're welcome."

I scoffed and leaned back. "You're such a bastard."

He laughed. "She's adorable," he said. I raised an eyebrow at him and he lifted his hands in surrender. "And she's amazing." I grumbled. "And she's half in love with you."

I shook my head slowly. "I…can't, Aries."

"Can't? Won't?"

"Can't," I growled. "She's human. She needs a human."

He smiled wryly. "Oh, the old eye for an eye bit." He lifted his bonded wrist. "Your hate for your brother's mate is showing."

"I'm sorry," I grumbled. He looked shocked and cocked his head at me. "It's not just that. It's not just that she's a human. She's…incredible. She deserves better. I'm a…demon. I don't even deserve to look at her."

When he stayed quiet, I looked at him and he was smiling barely. "Holy…my, my. I thought I'd never see the day."

"What?" I barked and let loose my glare on him.

"I thought you just wanted to mate her," he said with a wink and started to back up. "But Enoch Thames is about to get himself bonded."

"Don't even say the words," I roared and was breathing so heavy I felt lightheaded. But I didn't need to breathe. It was all in my head.

He just smiled and saluted to me as he walked away.

I couldn't let her bond herself to me. She'd be stuck with me forever, a murderer, a bastard. I couldn't let that happen.

My hands started to shake. I needed to feed so badly and this wasn't helping.

I lifted my eyes and searched for Franz. I was going to kill two birds with one stone.

Nine
Fay

When I woke, I expected Enoch to be there still, but he wasn't. I sighed, knowing that Clara and Eli coming in last night probably hadn't gone well and I'd just slept through the whole thing. When I got up and got dressed, I ask Clara and Eli what happened and instead of telling me, she immediately started telling me that he was just using me to get back at her and I should just go ahead and forget him. That he was going to hurt me.

So I rolled my eyes and left even as she continued to yell.

As soon as my foot hit the dirt and the sun hit my eyes, I saw Enoch marching across the camp. He looked like he was on a mission. I followed him to the big tent that was apparently deemed ground central for this place. Behind it was a community building.

When I got there a couple minutes behind him, there was a little group gathered there. They seemed to be getting ready for some kind of class or something. Someone hopped up in front of me and smiled really happily. "Hi! We're having a bow and arrow class. Would you like to join us?"

"Uh…" When I tried to move around her, she moved to block my way. It was the first indication that something was wrong. I did that uncomfortable laugh of mine. "What's going on?"

"Nothing? What do you mean?"

"You're blocking me? What's going on?"

She made a *pssht* noise and looked behind her. "Nothing is going on."

I put on my military face. "Move."

Her eyes got big. "Uh…"

"I don't know who you are or why you're…"

From behind her I could see Franz in the back hall, and he was escorting Enoch and a woman toward one of the back rooms. "That bastard," I whispered.

"He needs to feed," the woman blocking me said. "He's starving. She'll give him what he needs and then he'll be okay again. They'll be done soon and—"

"Stop talking."

I pushed her out of the way and ran toward them.

"I'll feed him." They all stopped, hearing me behind them.

"No, Fay," Enoch growled and came toward me. "I told you, I don't want to taste your sorrow."

I felt my heart beat hard against my ribs. "That's not the only way I can feed you, is it?"

He opened his mouth, but stopped. His eyes half-closed and he looked drugged. He sighed which turned into a groan. "Don't do this to me," he whispered in a beg. I leaned back a little, confused. He grabbed my arm and pulled me close. "You know what she's going to feed me, don't you?"

"Yes," I answered quietly. "You don't want that from me? At all? Not even after last night?"

"I've wanted nothing more from the minute I saw you," he growled, angrier than I'd seen him in days.

"Then what's the problem?" I murmured.

I saw everyone in the corner of my eye as they left the room, knowing this was no longer something they needed to see. This was no longer their business. Even Franz and the witch who was going to feed him left. She smiled at me as she closed the door. I didn't know what that smile meant.

"Don't do this just because you're jealous. You don't know what you'd be doing to me." He squeezed his eyes for a few seconds. "And to yourself. You might bond yourself to me." I felt my eyebrows rise. "Yeah," he prodded, seeing my reaction. "Then what? You'd be attached to me forever. An evil thing, a killer, a bastard who just wants to take your soul and keep it for himself."

"You kissed me once." I ignored everything else he said, because really, he was going to do anything and everything to show me the monster in him. Enoch shook his head 'no'. "In the water, you kissed me so I could breathe, remember?"

"That was different."

"It didn't feel different. The way your thumb moved against my cheek to calm me, the way you saved not only my life, but my sanity." I reached up and mimicked what he'd done for me that day, letting my hand cup his jaw, my thumb sweep against his cheekbone.

"Fay," he begged. "I'm trying to be the good guy."

"You're trying to be the villain," I said harder. "You're trying to show me that you're *not a good guy* and never will be. But that's not true. A good guy saved me that day, twice, a good guy brought me here and took care of me ever since. A good guy didn't try to kiss me or take advantage of all the alone time we had in those hotels and on the road and when we got here. A good guy took all the hits that people threw at him and let it roll off his back to save me." I moved the last inch, wrapping my arm around his neck, and let everything I felt come to the surface. All the hours of tension and want.

I knew when he registered it by the breath he sucked in. His tongue tasted his lower lip, but he didn't look happy about it. "Fay."

"Better than sorrow?" I asked and smiled a little.

I was doing this. He needed this and he wasn't going to keep me from being the one to give him what he needed. I wasn't just being jealous. Yes, that was some of it, but it was more than that. If he seriously thought I was going to sit in the other room and just *wait* while he and another woman came in here and…did whatever it was that he needed to do to get what he needed to feed, then he clearly didn't know me.

Why couldn't I just give him what he needed?

And why didn't he want it from me?

No, I was doing this.

I pushed up on my tiptoes and pulled him down to me at the same time. Right before our lips touched, his palm splayed out on my chest to stop me.

"We don't have to kiss." His voice was grated, his breaths loud. "I can feed from you just from thinking about it and talking about it. We don't actually have to—"

"You were going to kiss her, weren't you?"

He growled my name. "Fay."

He groaned the tiniest bit, registering my emotions, but I kept my face down. I had wanted him, but it hadn't crossed my mind that he might not want me that way. That was egotistical and stupid. He said he wanted me before, but why *would* he want me? I was a human. He was a creature with power. That woman that was going to feed him was a witch. He was probably pissed that the *feeler* kept getting in his way. I thought I had been right about the way we felt—he saved me, and the way he spoke to me and about me made it seem like his feelings...but I was wrong.

I backed up a step and took a breath, but before I could release the breath, he had my arm in his hand and was turning to press me to the wall. I gasped from the painful collision. He shook his head. "Stupid...human."

He moved so fast I didn't see him, and then his mouth was on mine, his chest pressing my back into the wall, his warm hands making trails across my clothes, but it didn't matter. I could feel his heat everywhere. My breathing was out of control, but it was moot at this point, because Enoch was grasping me tightly in intervals as he sucked in breaths and groaned against my mouth as he took my emotions from me. He tasted like mint.

I reached both hands up and gripped his hair, tugging, all the while turning to sit on bench, but he followed me down and hovered above me. He paused and waited there, his lips just out of reach, his eyes wide, honest, and open. I realized he was waiting to see if my feelings would change, if I was going to be afraid of him and he was going to be licking my fear from his lips instead of my desire.

I smiled just barely, biting the side of my lip. "I'm not afraid of you."

He sighed. "You should be. You have no self-preservation," he muttered and leaned in to kiss me, but he was smiling. I could feel the curve of it. With one arm bent at the elbow to hold himself up and the other hand coasting up and down my ribs at a torturous pace, he kissed me more gently than I could I have imagined being kissed from this gruff, coarse man who was so hell bent on telling the world he was bad. But right now, he was showing me anything but.

And he fed from me.

Every emotion I could muster in that moment I spared for him and pushed to him. He would suck in a deep, ragged breath, letting his fingers dig into my ribs gently, his hips and body moving and undulating with that breath as if it was guiding his very being. I could tell he was trying not to go too far, to keep himself in check, but he wasn't going to get what he needed if he didn't let himself go. He was an ornery beast when he needed to feed and I wanted that sweet man that I had glimpsed back. The man that I knew was in there somewhere. No matter how many times Clara told me he was a lost cause and a bad person, that he was just tricking me in an effort to get back at her—I didn't believe that.

I knew him somehow. I wanted to believe. I chose it.

The fact that he held back now instead of devouring me completely showed that he cared more than he wanted to admit.

I pushed his chest to push him off. He puffed breaths against my neck as he looked down at me. "I'm sorry. I'm sorry."

Even now he thought he'd gone too far. I shook my head and pushed him to roll off onto the bench. I crawled up to straddle him and he hissed his protest. "Fay."

"I love it when you say my name," I heard myself say. I didn't know why I was admitting that again; I just wanted to be honest. "Especially when you can growl it like that."

He groaned, cursing, and sat up, squaring me on his lap, a leg on either side, and put his hands on my sides. "Fay," he said— growled—causing me to smile. He rolled his eyes, but that turned into a chuckle. He cursed again. "You're killing me, little human."

"You know, when we first met, you used to say 'little human' like an insult."

He sighed. "And now?" he asked wryly with a little smile, knowing what was coming.

"Now you say it like you might like me." He stopped smiling. I took a deep, shaky breath and regretted my playful statement. He wasn't up to being playful yet, I guessed. "Never mind." I put my arms around his neck. "Just feed. We don't have to talk."

"You don't want to live like this," he said, almost so low I didn't hear him.

"What?" I whispered.

"You don't want to live like this, Fay." He looked right into my eyes, not hiding from me, and smoothed my bottom lip with his thumb. "You don't want to feed me your fears and lust forever. And hiding away isn't living, it's dying slowly."

"I don't know what that means, Enoch, but I do know that what I was doing before wasn't living. I think the way society says we should live is just stupidity. You should do what makes you happy. If you want to live in the woods, you should. If you want to move to an island somewhere by yourself, go for it." I looked down at his shirt; a couple of the buttons were slightly opened. "I just want to be with people who want me there."

He snatched my chin up. "*I want* you." He closed his eyes in aggravation. "That's not the point."

"It is for me." I moved closer, kissing his bottom lip.

"It's as easy as that?" He looked truly confused. "All the rest of it can work itself out? We're not even the same species. I'm a bastard, you're a princess. We don't...eat the same food to survive."

"Those things work themselves out," I promised and kissed his lips again, noticing how easily he was giving in, his hands moving down to my hips and pulling me closer. "If two people want to be together, they compromise on the little things. They make it work."

"We both like to sleep on the same side of the bed," he argued against my mouth and groaned as I began to feed him again.

I laughed. "That one is solved pretty easily." I bit into his lip and then moved to his ear, loving how hard his hands gripped my hips against him. "We'll just sleep on the same side together," I whispered before taking his mouth with mine. He was done fighting me and kissed me deeper and deeper.

He wrapped his arms tight around me, but still wasn't letting himself take everything I was offering. I wasn't sure exactly how this worked. I didn't know how long he needed to feed or how much, but I did know that he wasn't taking what he needed.

I pulled back just enough to speak. "Enoch, don't hold back."

He exhaled my name. "Fay."

"I don't want you to be in bad shape again because you were trying to be easy with me." He sighed again. "Look, I'm not saying let's throw down and have sex right here in the room while everyone waits outside the door." He chuckled and lifted an irritated eyebrow. "I'm just saying…I'm not a virgin." He seemed both irritated and slightly shocked by that. "You thought I was?"

"I…hoped."

I laughed reluctantly. "Hoped?"

"Any man—well, from my time, desires for his woman to be the only man she's ever been with. There's something very…primal about it." He cleared his throat, but continued to look at me. "But I'm not a virgin either, clearly, so what can I really say about it?"

"Well…it was one guy and—"

"I really do not want to hear about the human *boy,*" he growled, "who obviously didn't do a good job given the way your tone went down when you described the 'one guy'. And the fact that I want to find this *one guy* and rip his throat out for even looking at you, let alone touching you, when that job should be mine and mine alone."

My mouth was gaping, I knew, but I couldn't seem to shut it. Jealous Enoch was not only sexy but sweet and protective and strangely honorable. He put his finger under my chin and closed my mouth.

"You asked," he said in a low voice, a small smile on his lips.

"I don't think I did," I whispered back, a small smile on my lips as well.

"Maybe not," he conceded, and brought me down to him.

For the next half hour, he wasn't as careful with me and when he fed, I knew he was feeding for real. His lips were masterful, his tongue was an art form all its own, his hands were their own little playgrounds, and his fingers, extensions of his every feeling as they crawled over me, caressing and telling me things that his mouth couldn't or wouldn't.

We kissed like it was the last time and the first. He groaned so loud sometimes that I wondered if the others could hear him. No matter how carried away I got, he kept his word to keep me safe always.

We eventually leaned back on the bench and he held me on his chest. I went to move off, spouting some girly notion about being too heavy, but he shook his head, his breath moving the hair at my temple. "No, stay. I love feeling your weight against where my heart should beat."

That one statement changed my entire world. He had been trying to tell me that earlier and I had been so wrapped up in saving him that I hadn't *really* seen it. He didn't have a heartbeat because he wasn't human. I'd never have a normal life—what was considered normal to the world. Was I okay with that?

Yeah. I smiled up at him. Yeah, I was.

"What are you smiling about?" he asked and smirked up at me as his hand coasted across the small of my back and my behind.

"You're in a better mood," I mused.

"Was I so bad before?" I quirked a brow and he chuckled. "Okay. I know."

"Well, you won't have to worry about feeding anymore, right?" I asked and licked my lip nervously.

He gave me a wry smile. "You're nervous."

"Yes." My voice shook.

"Why?" he asked, and he sounded truly puzzled.

I gulped before I spoke and I hated it. "Because I'm afraid that you're going to go back to trying to hate me like before."

He nodded like he was thinking about it. "I should." My heart beat painfully. "I left Eli's house this morning with every intention of making sure that you—" He groaned as he registered my sadness. He rubbed my cheek. "Hated me," he finished. "I came here to feed on someone else and I knew when you found out about it, you'd be furious." I looked away, but he pulled my face back with my chin. "But you coming here was the best thing. You stopped me from being an idiot. I thought I was hurting you, hurting your relationship with Clara, hurting Clara and Eli's relationship, because I wanted you."

"Clara will get over it." I looked down and he must have sensed that I was about to get up. He gripped my hip tighter. "Why would you pick what was best for Clara over what was best for me?"

"I didn't. I didn't want you to have to choose. I didn't want you to fight with your sister when you just got her back. Finding her was the most important thing to you a few days ago."

"We weren't close growing up," I mused. "I felt guilty because of what I did. She's my sister, but she's not really my friend."

"I thought I was doing what was best for everybody." He scoffed. "No one wants Enoch Thames here. Trust me. They'd be happy to see me gone."

"That's not true. From what I've heard, they respect you."

"Yeah, like from your little talk with Aries," he grumbled. I smiled and shrugged. "Look, I'm sorry. I wasn't going to sleep with her, if that matters." I tensed and he winced. "Sorry."

"She was a pretty witch."

He grinned. "Most witches are. It's part of the package." He sobered and cupped my cheek. "I don't want to hurt you, love. The last thing I ever want to do is hurt you."

I smiled. "Then don't."

He laughed gently. "It's that easy, huh?"

"It's that easy." I leaned down and kissed his mouth once. "You're not a monster, Enoch." He tensed. "You're not a bad guy anymore. You choose who you want to be." He sighed against my mouth, all his pent-up aggression seeming to go with it. He sagged a little and I clung to him tightly. "We accept the love we think we deserve…but you're not a monster."

He brought his hand up to join the other and embraced my face in the warmth of his palms.

"I don't know how to be in love with you." He kissed my open mouth several times, almost like he couldn't stop, couldn't get enough. His shirt was fisted in my hands and I held on for dear life as I waited for him to finish that sentence. He leaned back and put his forehead to mine. "But I won't stop trying until I figure it out."

That answer made me ache in ways that I'd never ached before. I felt the tears come, but tried to hide them by hugging him around his neck. But that didn't work when he wanted to keep kissing. When his cheek connected with the wetness, he froze. He gripped my arms with me still planted firmly on his lap and leaned back a little. "What's wrong? What did I say?"

"Do you feel any sadness from me?"

He looked confused as he shook his head. "No."

"What you said....was..."

"Not the right thing?"

"It was the perfect thing. You can't feel happiness, and that's a shame, but if you could, this is what it would feel like." I put his hand over my heart as it beat wildly and kissed him like mad on that bench.

I knew that we'd have some people who weren't pulling for us, but I wasn't worried about them right now. We had a war to think about. The rebel camp were more lovers instead of fighters on a regular basis, so it appeared. They took in any rebels, any mated or bonded couples with humans, any creatures that were being chased by the Horde or other councils from their races for reasons other than lawful ones. This camp had over a hundred a fifty people in it. That was a lot of people to move at the drop of a hat, but as I listened to Franz in the big tent, it seemed this wasn't uncommon and they moved around a lot.

Everyone was present, so Enoch and I sat on the ground since there weren't enough chairs. When we heard the dinner bell, he had said it meant they were calling a meeting. Then he sat down on the grass and pulled me down into his lap. I had gasped at the move because, honestly, I thought he was going to be weird about it all. I never expected him to be so easygoing about us. He grinned at me over my shoulder and kissed my cheek.

"Close your mouth, sweetheart. The meeting's starting," he had taunted.

I had laughed and shook my head, elbowing his gut and loving the rumble and tremor I felt from through his chest from his laughter. Eli and Clara had come up not even a minute after that, and decided to sit a considerable distance away from us. I'm sure there were other watching and wondering what was going on with Enoch, but honestly, I tried not to look around at them.

Franz grinned like a goat eating briars at us as he started the meeting, and Aries and his bonded mate were currently sitting right next to us. Her name was Regina and she was this sweet and funny human redhead who would giggle and then look at Aries to see if he thought it was funny, too. It was freaking adorable.

The bond stuff was so interesting to me.

But for the moment, we had to figure out what to do— close up shop and head for greener pastures, or stay and wait for the rest of the Horde to show up and fight, knowing lives would be lost and bonded couples and mates broken, wait for the rest of Horde to show up and fight. Enoch wanted to fight, but I wasn't surprised by that answer.

"Our scouts have been hiding out and watching and those bastards are communicating with someone via radio," Franz told us. "They are waiting on reinforcements from the Horde. We don't know when, but they're coming. We know if we're watching them, they're watching us. If we make a move to leave, they make a move to stop us, so it would have to be in the middle of the night. No preparations. No packing in the daytime. No indications that we're getting ready to make a move."

"Franz," Enoch said quietly, but it still sounded so loud in the quiet of everyone and everything else. "I know this is how you usually do things—migrate from one place to the next—but wouldn't you rather just take care of the Horde once and for all so you didn't have to run anymore?"

Franz smiled. "Friend, there's always a Horde. Think about our history, think of all the times we've gotten rid of their leader. They've replaced him within a week and replaced all their ranks soon after that. As much as it…sucks for us," he looked around at everyone, "our kinds don't agree that we should mix. It's not just the devourer's Horde anymore." He looked at Enoch straight on. "The witch's Council has taken back up. And the Elves' Faction."

"What?" Enoch asked, his voice taking on that growl that I knew meant that he anger was rising. And his fear. "The witch's Council has been dismantled for…"

"I know. Over half a century."

"For this?" Enoch muttered and looked around. "For us?"

I looked back at him and smiled small at the way he said 'us'. He smoothed the side of my neck with his fingers, even as he went on. "No offense to anyone here, but what do they care about a hundred and a half of our kind mixing it up? Yeah, they don't like it, but really, we're way back out here in the woods. You're not hurting anything. You're minding your own business. It's not like you're trying to recruit Devourers to start dating humans and witches or something. What kind of damage do they think a hundred and fifty of us can do?"

Franz stared with a little smile that said Enoch didn't know anything.

"What?" Enoch barked.

"This isn't just one rebel camp," Franz told him. "When we saw you in Arequipa—that was our biggest camp. We don't know why, or what's going on, but in the past six months the amount of bonds, not just between humans and us, but between species to species has increased…exponentially. We have camps all over. This isn't the only rebel camp."

"How many camps are there?"

Franz smiled, seeming almost proud but also scared at the same time. "Eleven. For the moment."

Enoch's breath rushed out. "Eleven. Franz," he said and it sounded like a scold.

"We don't know what's happening. But *something* is."

"He said…" Enoch looked at me, his face hard and determined, but his eyes soft. "The troll in the woods told me this wasn't over. That the war wasn't over. He knew that they were planning something."

Franz nodded. "They are going to be hitting us harder than ever because our numbers are growing. We will fight one day, Enoch, we'll have to. But not today. Tomorrow night we'll leave and meet up with the camp in Colorado. We'll keep adding our numbers, growing our army, because that's what we are now. We're not safe anywhere anymore. The Consume Clubs. The Wall. There's a price on our heads everywhere we go. If they see a bond or a slash," he held up his palm, "they kill you on sight for the reward." I didn't know what that meant, but it was something significant because a lot of them started looking at their palms, like it was a precious thing. I took Enoch's palm and turned it over. He had one, too. I rubbed its length with my thumb.

I looked at him over my shoulder and he rubbed his fingers against mine as he looked back at me. More than anything else, he looked afraid.

"I brought you right to this, as fast I could get you here," he said quietly, and I got it. He was scared *for* me.

"They would have found me either way. There were looking for me. That's what he said. They were hoping to use me to get to Eli and Clara, and then get to the rest of the rebels. They didn't know that I was looking for her. You saved me by bringing me here."

He sighed, his breath hitting my neck. He waved his finger between us. "This is just going to make Clara hate me even more. You know that, right?"

I smiled and whispered, "She'll come around. I don't get it though. You came back for their wedding and everything. That was the last time they saw you since now?" He nodded. "I thought that would have made her have a soft spot for you."

"I don't deserve a soft spot. I was awful to her. Truly awful. I thought she turned my brother away from me. I thought she ruined my life. I thought she took everything away from me." He laughed a little. "I guess, in a small way, she did. Eli was already different before he met her. I hadn't seen him in so long. If it hadn't been for her, we wouldn't have reconciled. I sort of…owe her."

"But you said before that she hated you, and you hated her," I whispered.

He smiled. "That was just me, clinging to what I know is true. We'll never be anything more than a friendly understanding. I don't want there to be animosity, especially now, especially between you and your sister. Don't let this come between you."

"What?" We heard Clara's hiss behind us. I turned to see Clara and Eli had both wound up behind us. How long they'd been there was a mystery, but it must have been a while because Eli was looking at his brother as if he didn't know him, in a good way. Clara seemed on the fence, but before anything else could be said, Franz dismissed the meeting.

"Everyone get a good night's rest because tomorrow night...we're all going to need it." Franz came through the crowd and took the hand of a woman before coming to us. "Forget what I said about that good night's rest crap. We're having a bonfire and you're coming."

"Franz," Enoch muttered and shifted, but I was interested. I wanted to get to know these people. Who needed sleep anyway?

"Sure!" I grinned and grabbed Enoch's hand before looking back at Clara and Eli. "You're coming, right?"

"Uh..." Clara said with a grimace.

"Yes," Eli said and smiled.

"I think we've got some marshmallows in the community center. I'll go grab 'em!" Regina said and took off.

Aries cocked his head and grinned. "That means I'm coming." He patted Enoch's stomach as he passed. "Too bad you devourer boys can't handle a brewsky or I'd share."

"No thanks."

"You want one, Fay?" he called back.

"No thanks. I'll just stick with water."

When we got to the cabin, Franz had a large fire going. There were a few other people there, but not many. We all made a circle around the fire.

Franz's mate, who I didn't think was human, came out of the cabin with a couple of glasses. She handed one to me and one to Clara. "Where's Bridgette?" Clara asked her.

"She's inside." She nodded toward our cups. "She made these girly drinks for us."

"Ooh," Clara crooned all excited and took a sip. "Oh, my gosh. She's like a psycho in the kitchen."

"And that's a good thing?" I said with a laugh.

"Yes!" she said. "Taste it. Bridgett is a genius with herbs. She can heal you with leaves or make a smacking good lemonade." I sipped it, noticing the green leaf floating in the top, and was really surprised by how it tasted.

"Wow." I smacked my lips. "What is she?" I said carefully, hoping I wasn't offended anyone.

Clara laughed and looked at me over the flames. "She's human. But she mated a devourer." She smirked at my shocked look. "That doesn't happen very often. And she's lived with the rebels for a long time. Her best friend was an elf and she showed her a lot of the elvish ways with plants. It comes in handy."

"I got the marshmallows!" Regina yelled as she ran in with what had to be eight bags of them in her arms. "The fun can begin now."

Everybody laughed.

"Baby," Aries scolded and ran to help. "I told you I would help you."

"I'm totally fine."

"Yes, you are."

She giggled. "You got me with that one."

She tossed the marshmallows on the picnic table and jumped on his back. I laughed watching them and then turned back to the fire. I could see Clara and Eli so wrapped up in each other over the flames. He would say something low and she would rebut, and then he would say something and she would smile or bite her lip. It was so obvious looking at them that they loved each other so much.

She was toying with the buttons on his collar and his arms hung loosely around her hips. Every now and then, for no apparent reason as all, he would lean down and place a kiss on her lips, or vice versa, she would reach up and put a kiss on his lips. I turned my head another way to find Franz and his mate joking and kissing about something as he put another log on the fire.

I turned away from them all...right into Enoch. He was watching me and it was in such a way that I knew he had been watching me for a while. I propped my arm up on my elbow and nibbled at the pinkie nail of the same hand that held my drink. He watched that, too.

I offered the drink to him. He shook his head. So I tipped the drink up and downed the rest of it. His eyes watched my throat with great interest. I pulled him down on the log next to me to sit as *Monster* by Imagine Dragons began to play. We looked over to find Franz had turned on the mp3 player on his phone. He rested it upright against the porch and mouthed the words smiling as he looked at Enoch, like he was goading him. Or releasing him. *I'm taking a stand to escape what's inside me. A Monster, a monster...*

Enoch just chuckled and shook his head, apparently on to what he was doing. He turned sideways and straddled the log. He put his arms around my waist and tugged me closer until I was in the cove of his legs. I smiled a little and looked up and over at him.

"I *am* a monster," he whispered in my ear. When he saw me move to speak, he said, "But you make me feel like I could maybe not be one someday."

I bit into my lip and didn't know what to say in that moment. I didn't know how far he wanted to go with this. I leaned in and let one hand grip his neck, tugging and playing with his hair. I waited for him to show that he wanted me to move away, but he seemed the opposite. His hands on my hip pulled me closer.

I tugged his hair a little, and then his mouth met mine. He groaned in my mouth softly. I moaned back and hoped it wasn't as loud as it seemed. His hand moved to my back and then to my face. His hands were so gentle and tantalizing as they memorized me. When I pulled back and opened my eyes, his hands were still holding my face. I could see the others watching and they seemed confused or…mesmerized. Great. So I had been too loud.

I turned my embarrassed face into Enoch's neck and hugged him closer.

"Marshmallow?" Regina asked handed us a bag and a couple palmetto sticks. I opened the bag and stuck one on before sticking it in the fire.

"We ate a million of these when we were kids," I said.

"Never had one," he said and raised his eyebrow. "They look like a stupid food group."

I laughed. "You have got to be kidding me. Never?"

He shook his head with a smile. "Never, princess."

"We are fixing that. Right now."

He sighed and rolled his eyes. "I should have known I was issuing a challenge." He smirked. "So this is my life now. This is what I have to look forward to? You stuffing new things into my mouth to try and I pretend that I like them while you sit in my lap while everyone looks at us like a science project?"

I glanced around and everyone but Aries was watching us. He and Regina were focused on each other. I pulled the marshmallow from the fire. "Sorry," I sighed.

He scoffed. "Why are you sorry? They're looking because I'm different, not because of you." He pulled the palmetto stick up. "Give me that."

"No," I tried to stop him, but it was too late. He grabbed the marshmallow and mushed it all between his fingers.

"Ah, come on," he complained. "This cannot be fun for humans."

I laughed. "That's not the way you eat it, loser."

Someone gasped and I looked over on the log next to us to see one of the other couples. They were looking, watching, waiting as if Enoch was about to take my head off.

I groaned. "Go ahead, Enoch." I yelled louder, "Go ahead, Enoch, and rip my head off so everyone will see you for the monster you are." I laughed. "Over a marshmallow."

I could hear Franz and Aries laughing behind me.

Enoch grinned as he tried to wipe it off on the log. "You are so going to get it later for this."

I put another one in the fire and gave him the stick. "Hold this." I ran inside and got a wet rag to clean him up. He watched me wash him the entire time with great interest, his mouth slightly open. I took the stick from him and gently pulled the mallow off, letting it cool in my fingers. I took half the mallow in one bite and then told him to open his mouth before sticking the rest of it in his.

He chewed and I could tell he was processing. "It's different."

"It is," I agreed.

"It's good. Like a really sweet, disgusting pancake."

I laughed. "You're impossible."

Magic by Coldplay started to play and I leaned my head on his shoulder, but before I could get comfortable Franz's witch came and asked if I wanted to go for a walk.

Enoch tensed, which gave me pause. "No funny stuff, Soria."

"I would never," she proclaimed with a smile and took my hand. "Come. Let's have some girl talk."

"Okay." I looked back at him for a few seconds as I walked and he watched me the entire way. Franz went and sat next to him. Clara ran to catch up to us, along with Bridgette.

"Girl talk!" Bridgette yelled and it echoed against the woods. "Oh, my we need some girl talk." She looked at me dead on as soon as we were out of earshot of the fire. I could see her clearly in the moonlight. "Enoch. Spill."

I laughed nervously. "I don't know what to—"

"Don't do that. You know exactly what we want. Is that bad devourer a good kisser?" She grinned and bit her lip and she leaned closer.

"I'm gonna barf," Clara replied and half-turned away. "I've got a better idea. Let's play the who-can-talk-some-sense-into-Fay game."

"Clara," Soria chastised.

"What?" Clara replied. "It's clear that she's under his charms and she's going to get her heart broken when he's done with her and skips on out of here." Everyone looked at her. "What?" she said loudly.

"You really don't see it?" Bridgett asked softly.

"Whatever you're talking about? No, I don't."

"Clara," Soria began softly and crossed her arms like she was starting a lecture. "Okay, forget everything else for a minute but this. Who else *could* bring that hard butt down *but* Fay Hopkins. Your sister. You should be praising her skills, not just as a woman but as your sister! She tamed a beast!"

"I don't believe he's being true. It's an act." Clara looked at me. "I'm sorry, Fan—sorry. Fay. I'm sorry, but I think he's going to hurt you. He's very good when he wants to be. He's fooled me before. I don't think he would just flip his switch like that, especially for..."

I smiled. "For me, right?"

"I didn't mean it like that. I just mean that he doesn't like humans. If he was going to *fall in love* with someone, it wouldn't be a human," she finished really softly. I could tell she honestly, in her soul, believe what she was saying. She was trying to protect me.

"I get that you're trying to protect me, Clara, but I wish you could just be happy for me. I get that you were in this world before me and you think you owe it to me to like...shield me or something, but…" I looked over at Enoch and he was already watching me. I smiled at him and he smiled back before looking over at Franz who was talking wildly about something. "I'm okay here. I know there's all these things that I don't know, but you have no idea what my and Enoch's relationship is like. I know you don't trust it, you don't trust him, but there's proof that devourers change. You're married to one."

She shook her head. "That's different."

"It's not that different. Enoch was a devourer for longer than Eli, that doesn't mean that he's worse. You just didn't have to see Eli at his worst with your own eyes. You saw him when he was already changing, like me and Enoch. And that's a blessing, isn't it? We don't want to think about the person we're with as a monster, even though we know they're capable of it. If they choose to change, we should honor that. Enoch has changed and if you don't see it like everyone here is seeing it, that's fine. But I don't want to hear any more about Enoch not being changed, okay? I mean it, Clara."

She rolled her eyes and sighed. "Whatever. Just because I don't say it doesn't mean I don't think it."

"That's fine."

"So, now that that's out of the way," Bridgette rolled her eyes and looked at me with a grin, "is Enoch a good kisser?"

I burst out laughing and covered my face. They laughed and poked at me, saying that meant a definite yes. Even Clara was laughing and shaking her head.

"Let's just say," I told them, "that they don't call them devourers for nothing."

"That's true," Clara said and laughed looking at Bridgette and she nodded.

"So you're all bonded, right?" I asked. "I mean, I can't see them, but…"

"Not all of us," Clara said and glared. "And don't even think about it."

Bridgette laughed harder. "No, I'm not bonded, just mated to my devourer." She pointed to them. "And Soria is mated to Franz."

"It's all so confusing and romantic. Aries and Regina are bonded."

Clara crossed her arms. "How do you know all this? And how do know Aries?"

"After the shot the other day, Enoch got Aries to walk me to your house so I wasn't alone, and he could meet Franz. He was telling me about his mate and his bond."

She squinted. "That was the day that the troll took you in the woods."

"Yep." She pressed her lips together. "That was also the day that he was almost killed, almost stabbed by a goblin's tooth right in front of Aries to get me away from that troll."

"No way," Clara hissed under her breath.

"It's true. Ask Aries, he was pretty pissed at him about it. I didn't know that was the only way you could kill a devourer until after he'd done it and Aries was so mad, saying that he could have grabbed me instead, but Enoch wouldn't have it. He said he had to do it, that he couldn't let me be hurt."

Clara looked in my eyes and then back at Enoch. Enoch was watching us again and I knew he knew we were talking about him when he and Clara made eyes contact. She looked away angrily, but I didn't know if it was because her theory was dying or because she was still clinging to it.

All of a sudden, Soria gasped and grabbed her chest. She gripped onto Bridgette with her other hand and tried to breathe as…whatever it was kept happening. I assumed she was having an asthma attack.

Bridgette rubbed her back and said, "That's right. Just breathe through it." She looked at me. "She's okay. She's a witch, but she also gets these vision sort of things. It'll be over soon. It's okay."

I nodded, but I was on the verge of freaking out. Soria looked to the sky, leaning her head back and moaned. She cursed and grabbed her neck.

"Block her, Clara. Don't let Franz see," Bridgette hissed. "He always freaks out. She doesn't want him to see."

A few more seconds, which felt like hours, and she calmed, breathing in long breaths; pulling them in and pushing them out looked painful to her. She looked up at me and said, "Oh, God no. Something's big coming."

"What?" I asked.

She shook her head.

"She doesn't see," Bridgette explained and sighed. "She can't see a vision, she just gets an episode and knows something is going to happen. It's like a warning system, but we never know what to look for or when."

"But it's still really useful. We're on alert, if nothing else," Clara soothed.

Soria came to me and reached her hand up to my face. "Fay, I'm going to give you a gift."

"No, Soria!" Clara yelled and reached for her. I was so confused by the sudden turnaround of events that I just stood there. Clara yanked on Soria's arm, but she still reached my cheek and cupped it as if Clara hadn't yanked her at all. As soon as she touched my skin, I felt a warm wind all over me and then my eyes were opened to a new world.

I could hear voices and yelling around me as Franz, Enoch, and the men ran over from the fire, but all I could *really* see was Soria's face and all the magical, ethereal things that had suddenly appeared at her touch. The dark world was suddenly bright, almost like night vision. I pulled up Clara's arm from behind Soria and felt my mouth open as I stared. I pulled my fingers through the barbed string and it went straight through it. It looked like smoke. I followed it with my eyes the short distance to where Eli was standing next to Enoch, right behind Soria, next to Franz. Then I saw Aries' and Regina's between the two of them. My eyes looked all over for anything that wasn't normal, anything that I could notice and pick up for being different. When I saw the little jars in the trees, I cocked my head to the side and squinted at the glowing bugs in them.

"Security system," Aries told me and smiled. "They make a high-pitched squealing noise when anyone is moving about at night. Soria activates them with her magic before she goes to bed every night. But…humans can't see them."

I felt my muscles tense as I let my eyes wander and fall on Enoch. He looked epically pissed.

He growled his words at Soria, even though it was obvious to all that he was trying to contain it. "Soria, get your hands off her, give her back to me, and what the *hell* do you think you're doing!"

"Enoch, that's my mate you're growling at," Franz told him, a hand on his shoulder.

"Your mate just gave my mate the sight, without permission or cause or—"

"Mate?" Clara screeched. She looked at me accusingly, but I didn't even know how all of that worked, so I didn't know if I was his mate or not. Did he just say I was? Was there a ceremony? A bond or something? I didn't know.

All I heard was Enoch say I was his mate and everything pretty much stopped for me.

He and I stared at each other and he smiled a little in that *why does this always happen to us in front of a hundred people* kind of way. "Come on, Fay."

"What did you do to me?" I asked her as I went to him. He tucked me under his chin and wrapped one arm around my back, the other hand he used to lift my chin as he looked in my eyes. He sighed. "What?" I asked him softly since Soria didn't seem to be answering my question.

"I'm going to miss your blue eyes," he whispered and pulled my chin up higher to kiss me. I didn't know what that meant, but I clung to *this* moment, *this* second, as I gripped his shirt lightly and kissed him back. When he pulled back, I opened my eyes and immediately saw Clara behind him. She was covering her mouth, looking skeptical and peeved. I licked my lips and looked over at

Soria, who was being shielded by Franz now. He was wielding a wicked scowl.

"Soria, what did you do to me?" I asked softly. There was no nice way to word that sentence.

Franz grunted. She laughed and palmed his cheek, pulling him to look at her. "Oh, how I love it when you get all alpha male for me."

He tried to hide it, but he was practically a strutting peacock at her words. She kissed him and then looked at me. "I'm sorry. I wasn't trying to scare you."

"You didn't," I told her and smiled wryly. "I just...don't know what's going on."

"When I have a 'vision'," she said and made air quotations with her fingers, "it means something is coming like we told you."

"You had a vision?" Franz asked, all worried. "When?"

"Just now. It's not a big deal."

"But you hate them. I wish you wouldn't hide them from me."

"But you get all worked up over them and it's not a big deal. That's why I don't tell you every time I have one."

He sighed her name in a growl. "Soria."

"Baby," she responded with a smile. She looked back at me. "So we know something is going to happen. It's only fair that you have the sight if you're going to be with us, so you can be prepared."

"I think you should have asked," Enoch said hotly, but obviously less angry.

"I felt the need to give it to her and I follow my instincts."

Clara sighed behind me and I looked at her over my shoulder. She shrugged. "What? I tried to stop her."

"Why do you and Enoch not want me to have this sight so badly?" I laughed once. "It's something you actually agree on."

She shrugged. "I don't want you to have anything to do with magic, anything more than you have to. I feel responsible enough as it is that you're involved in all this and with…" She sighed again and cleared her throat.

"Point taken," Enoch said hard. "I don't care if you have the sight if that's what you want. I just wanted her to ask your permission first. I never want to force anything on you." He looked at me. Right at me. "If there ever comes a time that you don't want any of this anymore, just say the word and with a little persuasion, I'll help you leave it all behind."

Clara's gasp was audible behind us.

"Stop," I whispered. Begged.

"I'm just telling you the truth," he whispered back. He looked at Soria over my head.

I gripped his shirt in my hands tighter and blocked them all out. "What does the sight do?"

"Just that," Soria answered. "Shows things that are supernatural. Bonds, things that would normally be glamoured over to humans, anything paranormal that you normally wouldn't have seen before. A side effect of it, however, is that your eye color turns green."

My eyes were green… I was in this world now. I needed to have my eyes wide open. "Thank you. I didn't know about the sight, but I would have asked for it had I known it existed."

She paused. "You're welcome. I'm sorry. My gift chooses people and it isn't always tactful about it."

I wrapped myself around Enoch's arm, tugged him to follow me, and laughed nervously. "It's all right. Like I said, all is forgiven."

Everyone was more reserved when we got back around the fire. I could hear Franz asking Soria about her vision.

Enoch rubbed my hair for a minute and then turned me to face the fire so he could wrap his arms around me from behind. "Now you won't be cold," he whispered in my ear.

"You're being really sweet," I mused. "I'm fine, I promise."

"There's some scary things in my world. Now you'll see them all. "

"I'm sure. But you'll be there to protect me, won't you?" I couldn't help but grin as I looked up at him over my shoulder and leaned further into him.

He laughed into my neck. "Bloody hell. I'm done for."

"Bloody hell. I'm done for, too."

He bellowed a deep laugh and gripped me tightly to him. Clara and Eli were so fascinated that they did nothing but practically sit there and stare. So I ignored them. Franz and Enoch made up in like ten seconds. What would have taken girls ten months to apologize for took them ten seconds to take care of.

When Franz, Enoch, and Aries were talking about the next night and how we were going to get there was when we heard the scream come from the river. I jumped up from the log, but Enoch grabbed my arm.

"I'll stay with them," Aries told him as the other men ran off.

Enoch nodded to him and looked at me. "Stay here. I'll be right back."

He started to go, but I gripped his hand and brought him back to me. I went up on my tiptoes and grabbed his face to kiss him. I exhaled against his lips before letting him go.

"Be careful," I told him.

He leaned in and took one more pull from my mouth and walked away, looking at me as he did so. "A guy could get use to this."

I smiled and nodded. I hoped so.

We huddled and waited as Aries made a meaty wall of protection for us. It was quite comical how the men were so set on being the protectors over us without being asked. It was just in their nature.

Within minutes, we heard the crackle of leaves that let us know they were walking through the woods. We saw them emerge and I couldn't hold in my gasp as seeing a half-naked girl in Enoch's arms. He was carrying her, her arms around his neck, and I felt a stab of jealousy before I pushed it away. She was obviously in distress. Her clothes were dirty and her hair was a mess of wet curls, which meant she'd been in the water. I didn't wait for them to bring her to us. I rushed forward.

"Fay!" I heard Aries scold, but I kept going.

Enoch set the woman down and I realized he was carrying her because she had no shoes on. She limped a little in the soft grass and looked around at us nervously. Enoch glared at me when I emerged next to him. I smiled a little at him and shrugged, whispering, "You need a woman's touch for this."

I looked at the woman. "What's your name?"

She looked about ready to topple over as she looked at the ground. I saw the rest of them had followed me over.

"I have no name."

They all stepped back, apparently knowing what that meant. Enoch pulled me behind him.

"You're an outcast witch!" Soria accused and actually put her arm out in front of Franz.

"I am," she said softly. "I could have just not told you, but I told you the truth. Please..." she pleaded. "They stripped my name from me, but it wasn't my fault. Please." She fell to her knees and started to cry. Her tears sizzled in the grass and I stood in stupefied wonder.

I got a weird feeling about all this.

Bridgette was arguing with her devourer in hushed whispers before we could hear what they were saying.

"But everyone who comes here seeking help is entitled to at least a fair vote from the group!" she said and pleaded with him. "Augustus, please. What if they had turned me away? You would have never met me." She smiled. "And we both know how much of a shame that would be."

He shook his head and groaned. "It would be a travesty." He gripped her shoulders and kissed her before looking up and clearing his throat loudly as if to say, 'stop staring.' "She's right. We at least need to let the group vote. Our open door policy is what it is, but..."

"Why was your name stripped, and why were you cast out?" Soria asked, all business.

The girl's tears fell harder as she told us. "My clan was a very open and progressive one, or so I thought... My mate. I met him outside my clan and... He wasn't a warlock."

You could hear the sighs all around. "You thought they would approve?" Bridgette asked. "They never approve. What was your name before?"

"No," Soria said quickly. "She's never allowed to say that name again. We'll have to give her a new name."

"We?" Bridgette said with a smile.

Soria rolled her eyes. "She got kicked out because of her mate." She looked at the woman. "What was he?" she asked quietly.

We all noticed how she said referred to him in the past tense, and how broken up the woman was. It was obvious the clan must've not taken the news well. They killed him to hurt the woman and then cast her out. Wow, these people don't play around.

"He was a lycan."

"A werewolf?" Bridgette asked, her voice shrill.

"They aren't as bad as they say they are," the woman defended. "He was so good to me, and to them. He repaired things in our clan, houses that needed to be fixed, all kinds of things. They didn't even know he was a lycan until I told them he was. And then they killed him because of it. Because of me."

Her tears had made small black spots in the grass beneath her.

Soria knelt down next to her. "Our kinds don't understand. I'm a witch, too. I left before I could be cast out. I'm sorry we were so skeptical, but we have a lot of people coming at us right now. How did you even know where to find us?"

She gulped. "I cast a spell to take me to a place where I could be free." She shuddered through a sob. "I thought that when I ended up in the lake that I was meant to drown, that it meant that there was no place like that and death was the only option."

Soria hugged her, leaning away with a hiss when the woman's tears burned her shoulder. "I'm sorry!" she wailed.

"It's okay. You know how many times I burned my mate when I first got here?" She smiled. "A lot." They both looked back at Franz. He smiled as he came and helped her up.

"And I'd go through it all again," he said. "Come on. Come sit by the fire. We'll get you something to eat."

She looked back at Enoch. "Thank you."

He nodded once.

They all left, but Enoch grabbed my hand to hold me back. He sighed. "Having a strained, upset witch in camp is dangerous," he mused.

"Yeah," I agreed. "I can see why. But it could also be a really good tool."

"Witches are the most volatile creatures there are." He swiped his face. "I hope this doesn't blow up in our face."

"What happened?"

"She was in the water, so tired she could barely swim anymore. No idea where she came from."

I squinted and turned over what she said in my mind. "And you jumped in to save her?" I said, just now noticing that he was soaking wet.

"Yeah."

I started to walk back, but he grabbed my hand again. I smiled and shook my head. "You're getting insatiable."

The little smile that sat on his lips was adorable as he scoffed. "We haven't even brushed the surface of insatiable." He put a hand behind my head and tilted it back before bending down to me. I gripped his cold, wet shirt in my fingers. It made feeling his hard stomach that much easier. He shivered and moved a little. "I'm ticklish, love."

I laughed under my breath. "How is that possible?" I asked against his lips and kept kissing him. "I thought you were a big, bad devourer?"

"I *am* a big, bad devourer," he told me and before I knew it, a tree was pressed against my back. I laughed loudly and pushed against his chest and gave him a stern look.

"You're all wet."

His face twisted and he groaned. "Ah, you're killing me. Baby, don't talk dirty to me right now."

I giggled and had no idea why he was in such a good mood, but I loved it. I hugged him around his neck, not even caring that I was getting wet in the process, but apparently he did.

"You're going to get wet."

"It's okay."

"You'll get cold." He laced my fingers with his and tugged me toward the fire. "We'll get warmed up. Come on, princess."

I smiled to myself. "That name has really grown on me."

"I know." He smirked and looked over at me. "You never hated it to begin with." I let my jaw drop open. "I never got any anger from you when I said it. You've liked it from the very beginning." He leaned in and pressed his lips to my ear. "Admit it."

I huffed a laugh. "I will never admit it." I smiled as I stared straight ahead, but he looked at my peripheral and it made me smile wider. When we reached the fire, he sat on an open spot on a log and pulled me to sit between his legs.

The nameless witch watched the whole thing as she sat with a blanket around her shoulders, eating a bowl of something—stew probably. She seemed a little irked as she watched Enoch's arms go around me and settle on my thighs and I didn't get it. If she just lost her mate, how could she possible have a crush on Enoch already?

I got it—he saved you and you have some hero worship going on, but you said they killed was your mate. *Your mate.* Again, something wasn't setting right in my gut.

Enoch was looking the other way talking to Aries and Franz and hadn't seen anything. I was the new person in the group. Did I really want to be the one to start something by bringing up the fact that the new witch was crushing on my boyfriend? No. That's exactly what it would look like. It wouldn't look like a crisis. She caught me looking and smiled a little before looking away to finish her food.

"So," I started quietly so as not to disturb the boys' conversation. "What do you want your new name to be?"

Clara jumped in. "You look like a Marguerite."

Everyone just ignored that.

"I don't know, really. I haven't given it much thought."

"Who's somebody that you look up to?" Soria asked.

"My great grandmother. She died when I was ten, but I still remember her teaching me all the basics."

"Was there a nickname she called you?"

The woman smiled. "Violet—because it was my favorite flower."

"Violet it is," Soria announced, all proud of herself. "Finish your soup and I'll get you some clean clothes and a shower and a bed for the night."

"I'm done," she said and stood. She looked at Enoch and bit her lip. "Thanks again for saving me."

"Sure," he said gruffly.

Soria and Franz took her away and I turned in Enoch's lap. "Let's go get you cleaned up, too. I'm tired."

"All right," he agreed without a fight and waved to everyone once as we left.

He pulled his shirt off as soon as we were inside and kicked his boots off by the door. I stared at his back, at the muscles and scars and marks that living as long as he had had given him.

"I'm going to change," he called over his shoulder and grabbed some clothes from Eli's room before going into the bathroom. I figured I had enough time to change if he was changing, so I kicked off my shoes, and then pulled my jeans off and my semi-wet shirt.

I took a cami from the small pile Clara had given me and was putting it over my head when Enoch came out with dry clothes on. He was wearing nothing but a pair of jeans and a plain white t-shirt. I was never going to see him in anything but jeans it seemed. That was a shame.

"You're not going to put on something more comfortable?"
I asked as I finished pulling the cami down over my stomach.

"You mean like you?" His voice had gone deep and taken
that growly tone that I loved so much. His eyes looked at every
inch of me.

I turned to find something to put on. "I thought I had
enough time to get dressed before you came out."

I heard the swoosh of him blurring across the room a second
before he was wrapping his arms around my stomach. He pressed
his mouth to my ear and didn't whisper it, he growled it. "Do you
have any idea how beautiful you are, Fay?"

"No," I whispered.

"How is that possible?" He kissed the side of my neck. "Put
something on, sweetheart, because I want to kiss you all night."

I grabbed the first pair of shorts I saw and turned in his arms.
He leaned down and captured my mouth, tilting my head back
with his. His big hands grasped my sides through my cami and he
groaned as he picked up on the way he was making me crazy right
now. I had to admit that I didn't foresee that ever getting old—
being able to know, without a shadow of doubt that I was
attracted to him, and vice versa. Wow, that was an amazing
relationship tool. I grinned into our kiss and leaned up on my
tiptoes to reach more of him.

His hand, so warm it was ridiculous, crept under the back of
my shirt and pressed into my back while the other one gripped
my hip and then went lower to my thigh and under my behind.
He pulled back and licked his bottom lip. "You gotta put
something on, sweetheart," he groaned. "I can't wait to leave
here. We'll get our own place when we get to Colorado."

"We will?" I asked coyly.

"Yes," he barked playfully. "Don't even pretend like you don't want to stay with me."

"Colorado?"

"That's where we're going tomorrow night." He sighed and chuckled as his hands flexed on my hip. "Go. Now. Before I stop being the good guy."

I shook my head and slipped under his arm. "You've been the good guy all along, Enoch."

I heard him groan behind me and the bed squeak as I went into the bathroom. I brushed my teeth and combed my hair out. I even put some coconut lip-gloss on. Then I washed up a bit and shaved my legs as fast as I could because I knew that tonight was far from over. I smiled at myself in the mirror. Somehow, I had gotten what I always wanted. Someone who wanted me for me and didn't want anyone else.

I put the little cut off sweatpants on right before I walked out last and saw Enoch lying on the bed. His feet were dangling off the edge and I bit my lip at how sexy he was with his bare feet and his jeans. The trailer was dark, so he must have turned the lights off. In the small bit of light from the window I saw Enoch's face. He was looking at me, his eyes open wide, but he just lay there. It was a strange pose and a strange look on his face.

Something automatically struck me in my gut as wrong. His eyes begged me to run. I didn't know how I knew that, but I squinted and stopped where I was, looking around, completely silent. From the light in the window I saw it. There was a fog coming from the window. I looked outside and saw it everywhere. It travelled to every cabin and tent and spread out to every nook and crevice. It sought us out. I turned to it and it was coming toward me from Enoch through the kitchen. I knew I couldn't outrun it.

Enoch's eyes were wide. I knew there must be something in the fog that did something to you. Enoch wouldn't just lay there otherwise. So I did the only thing that I was trained to do.

I held my breath.

I shut my eyes tight and covered my ears and nose, crouched down, leaning down against the refrigerator with my back, and I held my breath with everything I had. The fog spread out through the house.

I waited and waited when finally, I had to see what was going on. At first I kicked myself, thinking I should have gone into the bathroom, but I saw the white fog as it spread through one vent in the ceiling and came out another. My lungs burned and ached.

I remembered when Enoch pulled me into the river and how he saved me by kissing me and giving me his breath. I wish I had his breath to save me now. He must not have seen the fog or not worried about it and breathed it in.

I looked at him and used his face to give me strength since I couldn't have his breath. He knew exactly what I was doing. I could see it on his face. He looked so proud and I didn't know why. I squeezed my eyes for a second and tried to clear my head. The fog was dissipating. I had to hold out. I fisted my hands on my knees and shook my head, refusing to give up yet. I could do this. I was trained for it. My head and heart were pounding so hard they hurt and my chest began to shake. I knew my body was going to start turning on me to protect itself soon. I looked at Enoch again and focused on him, on his purple eyes, and tried to stay calm for as long as I could. My chest ached. His eyes told me I was doing good. My lungs burned. I knew he was so angry, but he didn't look around—he looked right at me because he knew I needed him right then.

And then my lungs would hold out no more.

I released my air and sucked in air, praying it wasn't tainted with whatever magic was creeping over the camp. I waited as I coughed for just a few seconds and when I felt that I was fine, I rushed to Enoch. I hovered over him on the bed and saw that he could move his neck and fingers a little, but not much else. So he could have looked around if he wanted, but he chose to look at me because I needed him. I kissed him and it didn't hurt me a bit that he barely kissed me back. I knew he wanted to.

"Enoch," I whispered as I pulled back and cupped his cheek. "Are you okay?" I cursed. "I know you can't answer." I got up and went to look out the sliding glass doors. "There's no one out there. No one," I told him. "They must have all been affected by the fog." I sighed. "Eli and Clara didn't make it back." I covered my mouth and tried not to start thinking about what that could mean.

Enoch grunted. I looked back at him. He grunted again. I scoffed. "What? Stop being a baby?"

He made a kind of scoff noise and I tried to smile for him. I looked back out the door and gasped. "Enoch! That lying witch," I sneered. He knew exactly what I was talking about because he growled.

I shifted to the side so they couldn't see me and watched as Violet and two men I had never seen came out of Franz and Soria's tent. They started headed that way. "Oh, no."

I knew hiding was going to be useless. If they found me, they'd kill me. Besides—I refused to leave Enoch. I crawled up on the couch bed with him and faced him. He looked so worried and pissed off.

"It's all right, baby." He sighed at that and closed his eyes for a second. "I've got everything under control. I promise. I was in the military, remember?"

I took a couple calming breaths before leaning forward and kissing Enoch's bottom lip hard. "I just want to say that…I'm so in like with you."

He managed a small groan and his tongue barely touched his lip, but I got the message. His eyes held so much affection. I just looked at him, waited for the door to open, and tried not to show any real reaction.

When I heard the door open, I stayed perfectly still. "Two more in here," she called. "Ooh, it's the yummy one." She crawled up on his lap and straddled him. "Too bad you had to take up with this lot." She looked over at me with disgust. "And this human. We could have had some fun."

"He's not a witch or warlock," one of the guys she was with told her as he looked through Eli and Clara's things. "You'd be a hypocrite if you hooked up with him."

She leaned down to Enoch's face, her chest pressed to his. "Don't spout your hypocrite crap to me, Luscious. You have hooked up with almost every species there is."

"Yes," he said and I could hear his grin, "but I didn't try to make them my mate. You can't get all sappy about it."

She cocked her head as she looked at Enoch. She looked over at me and smiled. "I know you can see me. And you can't move.

That's got to be awful, and knowing that you let me come in here in the first place." She *tsked* me and watched me all the while as she leaned down and pressed her chest closer to Enoch. "You may not like it, but I bet he does." She grinned and turned to face him. "Gah, if I could have gotten one night with you, I wouldn't have wasted it."

When she leaned down to kiss him, I didn't know how I stayed still. I gritted my teeth and had to watch because I was facing that way. I watched as she pressed her lips to his. He was perfectly still, unable to move. She held his face and looked like she enjoyed pretending that he enjoyed it. She bit her lip and laughed a little to herself. "He's coming out of it a little bit already."

"How can you tell?" the guy asked her as he took something out of his backpack that I couldn't see.

She grinned. "He's fighting me."

That one statement made me infinitely happy.

"Let's go then."

She kissed him again and smiled down at him. "Bye, lover."

She climbed off and stood next to the man. "Is the Horde ready?"

"Yep," he answered and I could hear him straining for something. "As soon as we give them the signal, they'll come running."

She scoffed. "This was just too easy."

"They're just too *trusting*," he corrected. "One story about a dying mate and a poor little vexed witch and they welcome you right in. Stupid rebels. They deserve to die, every last one of them."

"And they will," she said and pushed him out the door. "Come on. Let's meet them at the community center and end this."

When she left, I sat up, expecting Enoch to be able to, too, but he couldn't. He could make his fingers move and his face could move a little more. He was so angry, that I could see, but there wasn't anything he could do about it.

"I know," I soothed and smoothed his cheek.

I laced his fingers with mine and put our hands on his stomach. His fingers squeezed mine. I looked at him and he tried to tug me down to him. "I can't. You heard what they said. They're planning something. They're going to kill everyone."

His eyes flashed and his lips parted.

"No," he said in a barely-there rasp.

"Enoch," I reasoned. "If I'm going to die anyway, I may as well die trying to save everyone. I heard them say the where and the when. I can try and—"

"Fay, no," he begged in a whisper, his eyes squinting, showing all the emotion that his body couldn't.

"I have to try. I have to."

He closed his eyes, knowing he'd lost. "Stay here with me."

"If I stay here, I die anyway." I cupped his beautiful face and smoothed my thumb over his lips. "I am so glad you saved me that day."

"Don't," he said hard. "Don't…say goodbye."

I didn't listen. I needed to say it. I smiled. "I'm so glad that you called me princess and danced with me. You made me feel like I was the only person the whole world."

He groaned as he tried to say something. "You…are."

I smiled and tried not to cry, but failed. "I am so in like with you."

His face twisted. "Don't do this, princess."

I leaned forward and pressed my mouth to his. I could tell he was able to move better this time. His lips caressed mine angrily and lovingly. I held on as long as I could, but I knew I had to go. As soon as I lifted, he pleaded in a growl. "Don't."

"I have to."

He was breathing heavy which just told me he was angry, because he didn't need to breathe. The blue veins were starting to peak and shimmer in his arms.

"I'll be careful," I promised as I put my shoes on.

He snarled as best he could, "You better." What else could he say when it was obvious that I was leaving and he had no choice.

I peeked out and didn't see anyone. I grabbed a knife from the knife block, opened the sliding glass door, and stepped outside.

"Fay." I looked back. "Stay calm. Devourers can feel you." I nodded.

"Okay." Although I knew that was a pointless venture because I was scared out of my mind.

"Deep breath," he urged in a husky voice that was coming back, "in and out. Think of something that makes you smile automatically whenever you're scared."

I smiled. "That won't be hard at all." I closed the glass door slowly and silently, and kissed my fingers before pressing them to the glass. He closed his eyes, as if in agony, so I ran.

I crept to the side of the trailer first and looked around. I didn't see them anywhere, but I didn't see anybody else either.

She had said they were meeting the Horde at the community center, so I went there first.

I passed Franz and Soria's tent on the way. I peeked in to check on them because I had seen the witch and the men in there. They were laying down on the blanket together. I leaned over them and could tell they both were shocked to see me.

"I'm sorry. I hate to leave you like this, but I'm going to the community center. They're planning some sort of attack tonight and they're going to kill everybody. I'm the only one awake that I know of. Enoch was waking up a little bit when I left him so you should be, too, soon."

Franz grunted when I tried to leave. "I can't stay," I told him. "They are planning something and I've got to see if I can stop it."

I didn't wait for anything else, I just looked outside and then took off toward the center. I checked in on Aries and Regina when I passed their place, but it was pretty much the same thing. Enoch was further along than they were, but I think that was sheer will more than anything else.

When I reached the community center, there were a few more men inside than I had seen before. The witch was there, too. She was the only female I saw though. I hid by the window and listened as they talked about when the 'detonation' would happen. My breath caught in my throat, but I breathed just like Enoch told me—in and out, slow and steady.

What were they talking about?

My first instinct was to run back and drag Enoch out of the house into the woods so I knew he was safe, but I knew that I couldn't do that. I would be damning everyone else, and could I live with myself if everyone else died?

I peeked back through the window. If there was a detonation going to happen, then they had to have planted something, and there had to be a device they were using to set the explosives off with. I crept around to the corner side of the building when they started coming out. Some of them had backpacks and I knew that's what they carried the explosives in. I remembered the guy rummaging around in Clara and Eli house and then his backpack.

I gripped my chest knowing that he'd put one of those in their house...where Enoch was. My insides warred with me, my heart pumped so hard it hurt in my chest. Go save Enoch or do this now and save them all. I couldn't not save my sister...

"We should have started using human devices a long time ago," one of them scoffed and I heard something bang near the window I had just vacated. "We would have won this war already and—"

I heard someone get slammed against the wall and barely kept my squeak silent. I looked over and could see their shoes on the corner of the building, not three feet from me. Someone was making gagging noises, like he was begin choked.

"Don't ever say you're happy we're using those feelers and their inventions for the cause. The only reason we are is because Byron is scared. Being scared isn't a reason to turn to the very thing we hate them for." He let the other man go and leaned away from him. "We hate them for mating with the humans so we go and use human weapons on them to end this war? No. We should do this our way. Take them out the good old fashioned way, but no, he wants to be a pus—"

"Marco," someone boomed and everyone got quiet. "Do you have something to say to me?"

The man sighed with a little growl on the end. "No, Byron."

"I am the leader of the Horde now. If you have a problem about the way things are being run, you come to me. If they want to shack up with humans, then they can die by human weapons." He chuckled. "I think it's very fitting. And no one suspects the Horde to be using guns and bombs. They won't even think the Horde is involved."

"Whatever you say. You're the boss."

"That's right. I am," he growled and slammed him into the side of the building again. "So do as you're told and stop disrespecting me."

When he walked past the guy muttered, "First we have to work with witches and now this."

"She got us in here, didn't she? She tricked them and then used her witchy fog, so just...shut up and do your job. Rendezvous point at the boat in sixteen minutes. Be done planting all the devices by then or get left."

The guy grunted, but said nothing. I leaned my head back against the building and cursed under my breath. Sixteen minutes. That's all the time I had left. The urge to run after Enoch got stronger with that knowledge. The urge to run and find Clara...

They had to have the detonator with them on the boat. Had to.

I moved to go and find this boat of theirs, when a hand closed around my throat. "What have we here?"

I looked at him and did the only thing I could think of in that moment. I threw my arm around his neck and used every bit of my feminine nature.

"Oh," I breathed into his neck. "Thank God you're here."

"Whoa," he said and eased back. "Number one, my name's Vander, not God." He grinned like the Devil. I tried not to vomit on him. "Number two, what are you doing over here, darlin'?"

I noticed how his hand tightened on my arm noticeably. My answer would condemn or save me, given by the way he was looking at me.

"I'm a witch," I whispered like it was a secret. "They were keeping me here against my will. Making me do all sorts of things for them." I showed him my palm. "See. I don't have a mark. I didn't want to be here. I'm not one of them."

His throat worked through a gulp and I knew I had him. He took my hand and rubbed my palm to see if I had covered the mark somehow. "What did they do to you?"

"You don't want to know," I whispered. "Mostly, they made me do things to other people, force me to make them talk."

"Those filthy bastards," he muttered. "Too cowardly to do it themselves." He took my arm. "Come on. I'll take you back to the other side of the river and you can go back to your family."

I sighed. "Thanks."

"You're awfully calm," he remarked and smirked as we walked to the back of the building. "I haven't picked up hardly any emotion from you."

"You learn to control it when you're around devourers all the time." I looked at him. "No offense."

He laughed. "None taken. You sure are a pretty little witch. Nobody tried to get frisky with you?"

I gulped and stared straight ahead. "A couple. One in particular. Enoch Thames? Ever heard of him?"

He scoffed a laugh. "Ever heard of him! Uh, yeah. Everyone's heard of him. He was here?" He whistled. "Whoo, that would have been a catch, boy! Too bad. I heard he was off the rails. We don't know which camp Eli is in, but it was rumored he was here. If his brother was here, it's probably true."

I shrugged. "Don't know him."

"They're twins, witch," he said with a laugh. "Getting Eli Thames in this deal will be a great prize for us." He looked at me. "You should join the cause. Especially after what they did to you. We're adding some witches to our ranks for specials missions. We could use your talents." He smiled, one side of his lips raising. "And we could get to know each other better."

"I thought the Horde was against witches and devourers...dating."

He made a *pfft* sound. "Who said anything about dating? I'm taking about having some fun. And the Horde is against interspecies mating and bonding. A little fun here and there on the down low never hurt anybody as long as you aren't flaunting it around."

I smiled and tried not to feel disgusted so he wouldn't pick up on it.

"Maybe," I muttered coyly and bit my lip for good measure.

He grinned and put his arm over my shoulder. "Ah, little witch. We're going to have fun together, aren't we?"

"I think so."

I breathed, in and out, and thought of Enoch, just like he told me. Not that he was in trouble, but I imagined his lips and his smile and his arms around me. Anything that made me smile. Enoch was right—in no time, I was no longer in the vicinity of angry. I was floating in Enoch and he was keeping me safe, even without being there. Vander grunted a little and leaned closer.

"Ah, little witch." His hand closed around my side and ribs. "What naughty things are you thinking?"

Worked like a charm. I smiled at him and looked around as I leaned against the tree. "I'm sorry. You just saved me and I'm...grateful."

He leaned his hand above my head. "You can be grateful all you want to."

"And I will be," I whispered, "as soon as we get back, I'll be *very* grateful."

I could see the boat behind us. We were almost there. There were about eight men there. Not as many as there could be. I sighed inside and had no idea how I was going to pull this off.

"I'll count on it." He took my arm again and pulled me along. "Come on. We need to hurry."

"What's going on?"

"Don't worry. They are going to repay them for what they did to you ten times over." When we reached the water's edge, he put his hands on my side and put me into the boat in one swoop. I gasped and he smirked as he climbed in. "Go sit," he ordered and pointed to the back of the boat. "We'll be leaving in a couple minutes."

I did what he said, but looked all around. And I looked for the witch, too. I knew when she showed up, I would be made and it would all be over for me. They would have to detonate it before they left the shore while they were still in range, more than likely. Things like this were something they barely touched the surface of in basic training for us. We learned the bare minimal and then they moved on, so I was going on what little I did know.

I huddled at the back of the boat and no one noticed me or seemed to care at all. And then there she was. She was coming over the bank with the guy she was with earlier. Probably planting more bombs. I closed my eyes and turned so she wouldn't see my face. Everything in my gut told me to jump off the boat and run to Enoch, but I let my eyes continue to search for the one thing that could stop this all.

Some of the men had walkie-talkies, some of them still had backpacks. I looked on the deck and the surfaces for anything that could be a detonator, but came up empty. I hoped it wasn't in one of the backpacks, but I figured they would want to have it handy.

And then I felt arms around me. I jolted, unable to contain it, and he chuckled as he pushed my hair to the side. "Is my little witch jumpy?"

"Yeah. Sorry."

"Don't be." He licked my neck a little. "Your fright tastes amazing," he hissed in my ear. "I'm sure we can work something out later on. I'm sure there's something I have that you want."

I tried to remain calm and breathe, just breathe. He was called away to do something and I gripped the side of the boat. I immediately turned my head to look around again. They were about to push the boat off. I had to find this thing. I was out of time.

I had failed. I had failed them all. I was about to jump off and run to Enoch, at least try to get him out, or die with him if nothing else—I wasn't going to just sit in this boat and float to safety—when I saw it. It was in the leader guy's back pocket.

He was on the other side. There was too many of them between us. And then they pushed off the bank. I breathed and thought of Enoch. Enoch's hands as they took my face and he looked down at me. I breathed in and out. I thought about Enoch's smirk, the way he glared at me when we first met, the way he was trying so hard to keep me safe and not let me fall for him. What a chore that had turned out to be. I smiled as I remembered our banter back then.

I opened my eyes and saw how far away from the shore we were. I was calm. No one was paying any attention to me because Enoch had helped me control myself. They all turned toward the shore and the leader reached back in his back pocket.

Before I could get scared and alert them, before I could think about anything else, I ran forward, snatched it from him, and bounded over the side. I dove down into the water with the detonator in my hand and prayed that I could figure out what to do next before it was too late.

Ten
Enoch

When I could finally move, I was so angry, all I could do was shake. My body let go slowly in intervals. My arms released, then my legs and the rest of my body. I was still weak, but I bloody well wasn't going to just lay there when Fay was out there alone trying to save the day.

I broke the sliding glass door opening it so hard, but trudged on. I didn't see anyone or hear anything. I didn't know what that meant. I blurred to the community center, but it was empty. So I blurred to Aries' and he was barely able to move. He looked surprised that I was.

"Have you seen anyone?" I asked him.

"No," he rasped.

"Fay didn't come by here?"

"Yes, she's gone—"

"I've gotta go, Aries. Sorry, mate. I've got to find her."

"Wait, I'll come!"

"I can't wait on you to get moving. Sorry."

"Enoch!" he called as I bolted and looked before blurring to Franz's.

Soria was up and trying to cast some spell over Franz. She lifted her hands up at me when I entered.

"It's me!"

She grimaced. "You almost got it, Thames."

"Got what, exactly?" I muttered. "Did Fay come by here?"

"Yes," Franz answered and looked up from the floor where he was sitting. "She wasn't under the spell?"

I shook my head. "No," I growled. "And I couldn't stop her." They both looked as I tightened my fists. "I've got to find her."

"She said she was going to the community center."

"I know. I went there. It's empty."

He frowned. "Soria, hurry, baby."

"I'm trying."

I asked, "What are you doing?"

"Trying to reverse her spell," she whispered with her eyes closed. Then she gasped and held her hands out to Franz. Her palms were bleeding. "It's done."

"I'm sorry," he told her and kissed her. He took her hands and wiped the blood on his shirt. "I'm sorry you had to do that."

She smiled. "It's the burden of being the camp's witch." She looked at her palms. "She knew I might try to take off the spell. She did that on purpose."

"I know." He helped her up. "Let's go make that witch pay for what she did. You helped her, fed her, and gave her your clothes and this is how she repays you?"

"I've got to go," I said and took off.

"We're with you," Franz told me and they followed me out the tent flap.

"Where's Eli?"

"Last I saw he and Clara were still at the fire. I don't know where they went after that."

I cursed and went faster, but not so fast that they couldn't keep up. We saw people coming out of their cabins and tents slowly since Soria took the spell off. They didn't know how it was over, they just knew they could move again. And then I saw Eli.

They were still at the cabin near the bonfire. He and Clara blurred to me and she was hysterical. "Where's Fay!"

"She…She wasn't affected by the fog."

"What?" She looked at Eli and back to me. "What do you mean she wasn't affected by it?"

"She held her breath. We overheard them talking about a plan… Whatever!" I boomed. "We don't have time for this. We need to find her."

"You mean you let her go!" she yelled.

"Clara, how the hell was I going to stop her when I couldn't move?" We heard a boat crank by the river and I knew then where she was. I turned to go in that direction.

"Enoch, wait," Franz said. "Let's think of a plan here."

"A plan?" Clara whispered. "What if they've got my sister?"

For once Clara and I agreed. I started to take off again and heard her gasp.

"Where are you going? You picked a great time to finally bail, Enoch!" I looked back to see her crying into Eli's neck. I didn't have time to reassure Clara. She was going to hate me forever. I was just going to have to accept that.

I heard them following through the woods behind me, but I was way ahead of them. When I reached the bank I saw the boat out in the river in the moonlight. They were talking and moving about. I couldn't understand a bloody word they were saying. I didn't see Fay. I saw the witch, but not Fay. I started to turn when a flash from the back of the boat moved and jumped, diving into the water.

Fay!

I didn't realize I had yelled it until everyone on the boat looked up at me. I looked at the rebels and saw they had already sent the cavalry. They must have heard me or seen Fay, too, but I didn't wait. I dove in and swam as hard as I could.

But I wasn't the only one.

A devourer, armed with a goblin's tooth in his hand, dove from the boat and he was going to get there first. I swam harder and couldn't see a thing in the dirty water. I used every sense I had, opened them up and let them guide me. I looked up and saw the faint shadow from the boat so I knew she would have dove and went to the west. So I moved that way and was rammed right in the ribs by the other devourer. Before he could leave, I grabbed a handful of his stupid, hippie hair and wrenched it to the side snapping his neck. I couldn't see the goblin's tooth anywhere, so I left it behind.

I looked around for Fay and saw a faint shadow of her. I turned her around and felt her fear hit me like a punch. She kicked at me as she tried to get away. I took her face in my hands, smoothing her cheeks to show her it was me. When she finally could see it was me in the murky water, her chest shook. I leaned in and once again opened her mouth with mine, pushing my breath into her mouth and lungs. I smoothed the back of her thigh, her side, and kissed her neck, just because I had to.

She was okay, she was alive…and she lifted a small metallic box in front of my face that I could only assume was whatever they needed to cause the damage they wanted to do.

I took it from her, put it in my front pocket, and kissed her forehead to tell her she did good. I turned to rise and check the surface to make sure it was safe, but was slammed again.

He took me down to the bottom and pounded my head into the rock before I could get a grip on him. He kept getting away from me every time I tried to grab him. I grabbed his neck and chin, but he was too far away from me to get a good hold.

I looked over at Fay and her eyes were barely open. She looked like she was floating. I roared and pulled the devourer to me, spinning us in the water so he was under me. He tried to grab me, clawing at my neck and face, but I plunged my fist into his throat, feeling his windpipe crush, and knew if he were human, he'd never recover. I saw a flash of dark next to us—the other devourer. I reached under his hand and didn't find it, so I tugged him closer. In his other hand I found the goblin's tooth.

He saw it coming when I raised it over him, but there was no escape.

I plunged in through his stomach and didn't stay.

I pushed off him and swam to Fay, scooping her up. I no longer cared if it was safe up top or not, she needed air and she was going to get it. I no longer had any. My lungs only held one breath and once I expelled it, it was gone.

We breached the surface and what I saw would have given me the warm and fuzzies had my heart not been dying in my arms. Franz, Aries, and the rest of the rebels had completely demolished the boat and everyone aboard it.

I swam and kicked until I got to shore. I yelled to Franz, "There's one more alive in the water!"

Clara saw me coming and was crying and saying things, but I was trying not to listen. All I cared about was getting this girl to breathe. I laid Fay out in the sand. Then I realized I was being pushed.

"Give her to me," Clara said. "Does someone know CPR?"

I pushed her away and put my mouth on Fay, just like I'd done in the water, and pushed my air into her lungs.

"Come on, baby," I begged. "Breathe." I breathed again into her mouth and again. I smoothed her cheeks with my thumbs. I realized we had an audience now, but I couldn't think about them. I had to think about Fay. Only her. "Baby, come on. Just like we did in the water." I did it again and again and again. She wasn't responding and her lips started to turn blue. I was getting angry. "Dammit, Fay. You just had to go, didn't you? I begged you not to. But you had to be the hero. Well, you did it. You saved everyone. And now you better come back to me. Do you hear me?" I slammed my fist in the dirt by her head. "Fay!" I breathed into her mouth once more, a long breath that turned into a kiss more than anything else.

I heard Clara start to sob behind me and then Fay coughed against my lips. I pulled back and cupped her cheek. "Fay?"

"Enoch?" she croaked and her eyes weren't even open yet. That fed a guy's ego, if I was admitting it.

"Right here, baby."

She smiled, coughed some more as she reached for me. I took her hand. "I love it when you call me baby," she rasped.

I laughed and sighed angrily, so relieved. I sat on the sand and pulled her gently into my lap. "You'll be hearing it a lot from now on," I whispered to her.

I could feel their fear and anger around me, but it didn't hit me. I wasn't absorbing it. It was as if this moment was the only thing that mattered. I didn't know why, but I was grateful.

"Did we get it?" she asked in a barely there whisper.

I assumed she meant that metal box.

"You mean this?" I pulled it from my pocket.

She took it with shaking fingers and looked at it. "This is a detonator. They put a bomb in everyone's house."

"So you really did save the day," I muttered.

"You don't sound happy about that," she said and looked up with a smile.

"I'm not," I barked.

"Me either," Clara butted in. I rolled my eyes as Clara moved in the sand in front of her. "What were you doing?"

"I had to, Clara—"

"Not you," she said and cut me with her eyes. "You."

I scoffed. "What the hell are you talking about?"

"Clara," Fay scolded. "He saved my life. Again."

"I know," she said in exasperation. Eli put his arms around her because it was obvious she was about to lose it. "I thought you were leaving. I thought you were going to leave this whole time, and you didn't. You stayed here and took all the crap I threw at you. You...jumped in the river to save my sister when that devourer had a goblin's tooth and could have killed you. I want to know why."

I sighed, hating all this touchy, feely crap. "I thought it was obvious."

"No offense, Enoch, but you told me once that you hated humans and their only purpose was for your food source," Clara said softly. I took it as a good thing that Fay didn't flinch at least.

Before I could defend myself, Fay spoke. "I know all about it. He told me he hated humans. He's told me everything."

She squinted. "Then how can you—"

"Love changes things," I interrupted. Everyone stayed quiet after that. "From the minute I saw you," I told her, no longer speaking to Clara. I let everything go as I turned her on my lap to face me. I looked into her green eyes and mourned for those blues I'd never see again as I let my thumb love on the skin of her jaw. "I knew you were going to be different. That's why I fought it so hard. I knew you were going to wreck me. And I hated you for it." She smiled. I knew she would. Clara looked between us and shook her head, so not getting it, but my Fay got it and that's all that mattered. "I hated you and wanted you so badly all in the same breath." She gripped my wet shirt in her fingers. "I was already changing before I met you, for better or worse, but you were the final nail in the coffin. You destroyed the man I used to be," I took her face in my hands, "and I'm falling for you more and more for it."

Clara made a noise in her throat.

Eli wrapped an arm around her shoulders. "CB," he whispered, "Why are you being so hard about this?"

"Because if he's going to be in this family then he needs to be in it for good! I don't want to worry about him taking off or getting pissed off for no reason and leaving Fay. Or us," she said and promptly burst into tears. Fay and I looked on confused as Eli tried, futilely, to console her.

"What's it to you, Clara?" I said carefully. "You hate me anyway."

She sniffed and looked up at us. "I'm…pregnant, Uncle Enoch." She swung her gaze to Eli. "I'm pregnant. I'm sorry."

His mouth was slightly open in shock, but I had to give it to him. He swung back into action quickly, though he looked like he could keel over. "You are? How far?"

She dropped her chin. "At least seven weeks."

"Clara," he scolded, a growl tacked on.

"I'm sorry," she sobbed and covered her face. "I know that the Horde is onto us so heavy and…" she looked up, her face covered with tears, "and I'm carrying the one thing they despise most. The thing they are trying their hardest to stop." She looked at me. "The one thing *you* despise. At least…that's what I thought. I was afraid to say anything, especially with Enoch here. I didn't know if this thing with Fay was all an act or not. I couldn't risk it."

I felt true guilt for the second time in my life as I watched my brother hold his scared-out-of-her-mind wife and knew that the reason she'd been so protective and seemingly over the top wasn't just because she was a sister protecting her sister—though it was that—was she was a mother protecting her child. And she had good reason.

Once the Horde found out that Eli Thames was having a child with his human bride, the bidding wars would start for the reward to whoever brought them down. I shook my head.

That troll hadn't realized how right he had been.

This war really was just beginning.

Eli held her close and lifted her chin. He smiled. "Don't you dare. Don't you dare make this something bad. We're going to have a baby, Clara." He kissed her and wiped her cheek. "Remember, on the boat to Arequipa, you told me you wanted kids and a white fence?" She gave him a half smile. "Well, this is half come true."

She laughed reluctantly. He wrapped her arms around his neck and lifted them from the ground to hug her tight, but I saw it. Behind her back where she couldn't see, he was afraid. He gripped her back tight and looked like a man who was about to lose the one thing he wanted in the world. He was a human now. He couldn't protect her, and as much as he may have hated that fact, it was the truth.

I don't know why he looked at me then, but he did. I nodded, letting him know that I wasn't going anywhere. They had to know that by now, right? I basically professed my love for Fay in front of everyone. Well, not everyone.

I looked around and saw Aries and Franz and the rest of the men piling the bodies up.

"Are you okay? Did the smoke, fog, whatever hurt you?"

I looked back to find Eli kissing Clara, making it impossible for her to answer.

I looked away from them and took Fay's chin in my fingers, pulling her to look at me. "Are *you* okay?"

"I'm fine. Now."

"What happened?"

She sighed and pushed her wet hair back. "I'll tell you about it later, okay? Right now I just want to be here." She laid her head in the crook of my neck and settled against my chest. She was shaking and I wrapped my arms around her small frame, tucking her in closer for to my warmth, but also for my primal need to have her close.

"You almost died," I growled, all my anger coming back. I knew the blue veins were showing in my arms and neck, but I couldn't stop. "You lay there and I thought you were going to die, just like that. Human life is so fragile and I hate that you can be taken from me so easily." Her fingers ran across the blue veins on my arm and hand lightly. "But if you hadn't been human, I wouldn't have fallen for you."

She smiled in her peripheral. "You didn't date witches and pixies?"

"No," I groaned and tugged her closer. "I didn't date witches and pixies. I was only ever with…humans. I was never even with devourers. That doesn't even make sense." I laughed once.

She turned her head, letting me see her eyes as she searched my face. She touched my neck and jaw. "These will heal, won't they?" she asked of the scratches I got from the devourer in the river.

I nodded. "Yeah. I always heal."

She bit into the side of her lip and my gut went crazy. She draped one arm around my neck and rested her face back into my neck. Eli and Clara were still preoccupied with each in whispers and if I saw him grab her stomach one more time… I rolled my eyes and smiled. My brother, the father. It suited him.

I realized that I hadn't ever moved on to any other species because I had been waiting for Fay. She had been meant for me all along. If there was one person out there for one other person, she was mine. I had become a complete sap, the thing I hated, the person I resented and made fun of, that was me. I grinned and shook my head.

And I was going to be an uncle.

And that thought actually didn't make me want to vomit.

I kissed Fay's forehead and thought she might be asleep, and I wouldn't blame her a bit after the day she had, but I still had to say it. "You're mine now, princess."

"And you're mine," she answered and I felt her smile against my neck. I felt something a little warm around my heart, but I just pulled her chin up and lowered my mouth to hers. I exhaled against her skin, claiming her. She licked her lips as I pulled back. She was mine, my mate, my *whatever* you wanted to call it.

I looked around at the camp and knew exactly that we had to do. I pulled the detonator from her lap and we looked at it. She realized it, too, and sighed roughly as she nodded.

"Yeah," she said.

"Everybody okay?" Franz yelled as they finally made their way over. A large pile of bodies burned near the river. The boat was gone, too. I assumed he sank it.

I stood with Fay in my arms and let her feet touch the ground. Franz and Aries were looking at her like she hung the frigging moon. I groaned a little, but it sounded like a growl more than anything, and Aries laughed. Franz rolled his eyes at me and grinned at Fay. "You did good, girl."

"I just did—"

"You just saved everyone's lives," Soria's said and scoffed while she cried and wiped her eyes. "That's all."

"We need to get our belongings together," Franz told everyone.

I nodded and lifted the device. "We need the rest of the Horde to think they succeeded."

Franz nodded and looked at Fay. "You know how to use that thing?"

"They put devices in all the houses to explode," she explained. "So when you press this button, it'll detonate the explosives."

"It's that easy?" I asked and shook my head. "Press a button and everything blows up? Humans make things way too simple. But…it just can't be that easy, can it?"

"Sometimes," she leaned in and whispered, "we accept that it's just that easy."

———————

I laced my fingers with hers as we stood on the bank of the river, having done a head count and made sure everyone was accounted for several times before the button was pressed. Then the safety cap was removed, Franz pressed the button, and we all watched as the camp they'd lived in for months was demolished, leveled to nothing but fire and smoke.

Not many of them got sappy about it. They were nomads, travelers, gypsies, so they knew that a move was always on the horizon. What surprised me most was how we were going to get to Colorado. I had wondered what happened to the car I stole since we arrived, but hadn't wondered enough to actually ask, but as we all trekked through the woods, the long way around the river to the other side, I saw how they were going to get us there.

And I saw the stolen car they had *stolen* from me.

I smirked at Franz as he passed me with a little devious smile.

They had a few vans and trucks, there was even two old yellow school buses.

Franz shrugged. "You leave them by the side of the road unattended, it's fair game."

"A school bus is fair game?" I laughed. "I find it hard to believe you weaseled two buses away without anyone noticing."

"I bought them," Eli said as he passed and shook his head.

"Don't take my fun, Thames," Franz grumbled.

I laughed and hoisted Fay into my arms, blurring her to the car we had stolen. "Dibs," I whispered into her hair.

She tried to grin, but it was tired. I could tell she was so tired. Dying on a beach and being brought back to life would do that to anyone. I held her face and kissed her once before I put her on the seat and called Eli's name. I nodded for him and Clara to ride with us.

When I climbed in, I tugged Fay's sleeve so she would lay her head in my lap. She sighed so contently and I felt that bone deep satisfaction once again. For a moment, all was right in the world.

And then Clara leaned over the seat.

"I'm glad I was wrong about you," was all she said before she kissed my cheek and leaned back. I was shocked that I didn't want to punch something. Maybe Clara and I might...maybe....could be friends after all.

"Um...are we gonna go?"

I shook my head. No. No, we were never going to be friends.

"I'm driving," I threw back at her and started the car with a chuckle. "You just sit back and enjoy the ride, prego."

"Oh, you are most certainly not calling me that."

Fay laughed from my lap and rubbed my thigh.

"Oh, boy," she muttered and snuggled in closer as she tried to go to sleep. I rubbed her head and neck, knowing the next eleven hours of driving were going to be long, but the girls would sleep through most of it. I was actually looking forward to talking to my brother. Never thought that day would come.

"Baby," Eli said.

"What?" she said, the exasperation in her voice clear.

"Go to sleep," he ordered softly.

Anyone else would have been chopped in half by her sharp tongue.

She sighed. "Okay." She laid her head on his shoulder, but he pulled her down to his chest instead and leaned against the door, propping his feet up on the seat with her.

"Just go to sleep, love. Where do you want to go?"

I rolled my eyes, knowing right then that I wasn't getting to talk to him at all if he was taking her in reverie. But then I squinted. "Wait, you're human."

He smirked. "Not all."

"It's okay," she yawned her words. "I think your big brother wants to talk anyway."

I smiled. She remembered that I was the oldest by six minutes and she was perceptive enough to know I wanted to talk.

He started to hum a little against her forehead and I felt a crack go through me. It was painful enough that the car swerved a little. Eli's eyes opened, but he didn't move. "You all right?"

"Fine," I answered gruffly.

But I wasn't. My chest and stomach were on fire. I drove on and eventually it subsided to a dull ache. The girls were asleep, but Fay was murmuring my name. I kept rubbing her hair. I didn't know if Eli could hear it or not. If he did, he said nothing.

Eli went ahead and hit me with the sledgehammer. "You want to know if what happened to me is what's happening to you."

"It doesn't make sense." I didn't waste any time so I didn't chicken out. "I didn't want to be like you. I wanted to be a devourer. I don't know why things are changing. I tried to fight it, with everything in me, but now…I wouldn't change anything. I wouldn't go back." Fay's silky black hair combed through my fingers and I didn't deserve her. "I feel like it doesn't belong to me."

"I think that's the difference. You *feel*. What does Fay say about it?"

I scoffed and smiled as I drove on.

"For humans, everything's easy. If you want to change, change. If you want to be forgiven, ask for forgiveness. If you want to be someone different, then don't be the same man ever again." I gulped. "That's what I did. That's what I'm doing."

Epilogue
Fay

We arrived at the Colorado camp the next day and they were prepared for us. They had a big dinner ready of soup and sandwiches. Their accommodations were a bit more primitive than the other camp we had been renting. This was all tents, no cabins or buildings of any kind, except showers and bathrooms. I sighed and it must have been louder than I thought. Enoch put his arm around my shoulder and brought my head closer.

"We can always hit the road again and do the motel circuit."

I laughed. "That's not sounding too bad."

"Hey," Clara scolded and looked around. "It's totally secluded. It'll be like all those trips we took with Mom and Daddy to Little Bitterroot Lake. All we need is a tire swing and bugspray."

Enoch scoffed. "And some root beer and corn on the cob and a toothpick, right?"

She squinted her eyes and punched his arm lightly as they walked by. "You're going to be perfectly fine here. Even you can have fun at a bonfire. I've seen it." She turned back to look at him. "Or was it just my sister's influence?"

"It was just your sister," he said and smirked, pulling me closer by the arm around my neck.

She rolled her eyes and gripped Eli's hand as he laughed. They met everyone at the fires they had going and sat in the grass. It was dark, but they had tents set up and I was grateful. It was a lot of people in one place. A lot. It felt like boot camp; long lines and loud conversations. We sat with our group around a fire and the boys went off to have a meeting with the leaders of the camp.

When Clara was talking with Bridgette about something, I turned to Soria and Regina. "Regina, will you tell me about your bond?"

She smiled and rubbed her wrist. "Aries was shocked."

"How come some people have them and some don't?"

Soria grimaced. "Franz actually got upset, thinking that I didn't want him enough. But it's not really my choice. It's something inside us, something that's not really in our hands. You choose to bond before you even decided to." She smiled. "It doesn't mean I love him any less. I tried once, to bond myself to him. I tried so hard, but it wouldn't work." She shrugged. "Like I said, it's something inside our very souls that decides, not us."

"Wow," Regina sighed, "that's really beautiful."

"Shut up," Soria said and shoved her.

"So," I swallowed and clasped my hands behind my back, "you're saying I have no choice?"

"You've already decided." She smiled in a knowing way.

I gasped, barely. "Do you...know something?"

She scoffed. "I can't tell the future. I wish."

I rubbed my neck and pressed my lips together. "Thank you, by the way. If you hadn't given me the sight, I never would have seen the witch's fog and been able to avoid it."

"Yeah," she stalled and paused avoiding my eyes. "You saved us all. We should be thanking you."

Regina hugged me. "So glad you're all right. And don't worry about the bonding, mating thing. It'll happen in its own time." She pulled back, but left her hands on my shoulders. "And I know Enoch slipped up and said 'mate' that one time, but just wait 'til he tells you that you're *his*. Ahh," she groaned. "When you know you're his and no one else's, you're his mate and then you have nothing to worry about."

I squinted. "Uh..."

"You're mine now, princess."

"And you're mine."

"What?" she asked, seeing the look on my face. She grinned. "What!" she whisper-shrieked.

"I think we already did that part." They both gasped and leaned in. "On the beach, right after he saved me. He said 'you're mine now' and I said 'and you're mine'. Does that mean...?"

"Yes!" they both squealed and tackled me in a group hug. "Ohmigosh!" and "You're mates!" and "So sweet!" were all mixed together in a jumble.

"Wait." I stopped them, unable to let the happiness bubble over if it wasn't true. "Are you sure that's what it means."

"If that's what he said, that's what it means," Regina answered. "Mine means *mine*. Mine means *his*. That is the word he would use to claim his mate. He may not have had the official talk with you because, yo, you just died and all, but you're totally mates."

Clara joined the group with a curious look on her face and I was worried she'd be angry. We'd never been close. Even as teenagers, we'd always been more the sisters that fought and avoided each other than the kind that stuck together and did things. When it got quiet, she knew it had to do with Enoch. She made a sulky face, but smiled. "What is it? I can take it."

"Enoch..."

"What?" she asked.

"I made Fay my mate." I whipped around at the sound of Enoch's voice to find him there with a smirk on his face. "That is what we're talking about, right, ladies?"

I didn't know what to say so I just stared. He was alone and his smile was soft as he made his way to us, his steps silent in the grass but strong, and they made his entire body shift. I gulped, suddenly not sure what to do with this man who was stalking over like a panther. His gaze never left mine until he reached me. He handed Clara and me a mug of something.

"Hot chocolate," he told us. "Eli and the rest of the guys are coming. Sorry, girls. I only had two hands, but I know I saw Franz with some mugs so I'm sure some is coming for you," he told Soria and Regina with a wink.

"That's okay," they said dazedly. I laughed under my breath.

"So, you hate me again?" he asked Clara.

"Why?"

"I stole your sister," he told her, but looked down at me. She shrugged. "So we're even."

I could hear the river as he tugged me along. It was dark, but the moon was so bright. I looked back and could see tents everywhere. The Colorado group only had about thirty to begin with, so we were the bulk of their mass. Clara had said that Eli and Franz's money funded most of the cause. And I knew Enoch had money, too, though I had no clue as to the extent of it. Some of the fruits of that money were in my hand. He wouldn't take no for an answer.

I had a backpack full of clothes and stuff I'd need, as did Enoch. We stopped on the way and got some necessities. We were going to be camping after all. For how long, no one knew. We had spies and eyes out looking for word from the Horde and the new councils with the witches and the elves.

Things would get worse before they would get better.

"Hey." I turned to look at him. He was serious and gruff, worried. "You all right?"

I nodded. "Yeah." I half-smiled, holding my sleeping bag to my chest tight. I went ahead of him in the tent and kicked my shoes off outside. I laid my sleeping bag out, unzipped it and, opened it up. He was kneeling beside me, watching me. "If you put yours on top of mine, then we can zip them together and we'll both fit."

He sighed. "You want to sleep with me?"

I blinked. "You don't?"

He chuckled and leaned in to hug me to him. "Of course I do. I just never got to talk with you and when Clara asked me..." I leaned back just enough to look up at him. "I wasn't sure if you were going to be upset with me about saying you were mine." I shivered. Regina was right. Hearing I was *his*... He groaned, but that swiftly moved into a husky chuckle that he pressed to my ear. "Ah, my little human, you're killing me."

"No," I told him, but it came out as nothing but breath. "I'm not angry."

"You stalled outside the tent." He paused. My Enoch was unsure. "I thought it might be that I claimed you and had not discussed—"

"I'm yours." I looked up so he could see my eyes. I knew right away he was mourning my blue eyes, but what I saw in his face couldn't be real. He had said before that love changed things. He hadn't said he loved me, but I think it was obvious that we were well past like. You know when you're on a course that you know is the right one. You can't explain it, you can't define it, you don't know how you got there or what all the obstacles will be, you just know the end result will be amazing and it will be worth it.

That was the road I was on.

Full speed ahead, no blinkers or turn signals, just cruise control.

He cupped my face and didn't ask, he took. *This* was the Enoch I knew. He pushed the backpack from my shoulders and tossed it in the far corner. He pulled away to reach over and zip the tent up. When he returned, he grinned cockily as he took my face again.

"See, didn't I tell you I'd get us our own place."

I nodded with a smile and tugged him closer with his shirt. He groaned as we crashed together. I knew with everything that had been going on, he hadn't fed in a while. He hadn't said anything, but I was beginning to notice the little signs. I let everything come forward, all my feelings for how he saved me, how he cared for me so obviously, how he pushed all his old self away the past few days and really stepped up to show me how much he wanted me, all of it.

He sucked a breath against my lips. "You don't have to do this."

"I'm just being me."

He chuckled in that way that said he was annoyed. "You are so going to be a handful." He swept my hair back. "My little beautiful handful." He sighed. "I can wait. I know what you're doing. You're pushing extra hard to feed me. You've been through so much..." he looked down at my neck as if he couldn't stand to think about it, "...the last couple days and I can wait." He looked back up at my eyes. They were harder. "Besides, I don't want you to think this is just me needing to get my fix all the time. I want to touch you because I want to touch you, not just because I need to feed."

I nodded. "And you don't think I want you to touch me?" He paused, still. "You don't think that when you touch me it doesn't make me insane?" I breathed. His eyes became a little more lidded as he watched me. "You don't think that when you look at me like that I don't want you to kiss me? To put me on your lap and make me sit there for hours?" He gulped. Actually gulped. I felt so much triumph. "The goal is to kiss you, Enoch." I pushed my arms around his shoulders and kissed his neck. He groaned, the tiniest moan. I moved up on my tiptoes and faced him. "It's my honor to give you what you need, but the goal is to touch you. Feeding you in the process is just a perk."

I felt his hands on the backs of my thighs before he lifted.

"You aren't real, Fay," he whispered harshly against my mouth.

I wrapped my arms all the way around his head, bringing us as close as we could get. I loved feeling his hands on my legs and our bodies pressed together all the way down, warm and right.

"I'm real. And I'm yours."

"Gah, I love to hear you say that you're mine," he growled. We laughed into our kiss, but his kiss was barely a whisper as he lowered us down to the sleeping bag. "You know I'm asking for forever, right?" His eyes closed for a moment and I knew exactly what he was thinking. "As forever as human life will let us have."

When he opened them, he tried not to let me see, but it was hard to hide the pain there.

"Forever is what I want," I whispered.

It had crossed my mind, too. Of course it had with all the thoughts of the bonds. But with the way this life was going, we didn't know what was going to happen. I almost died yesterday. Who knew if I would even make it to fifty. I wasn't wasting time worrying about that.

Apparently, neither was he.

"Come here, little human," he ordered, cupping my chin and pressing me into the blanket. "No more talking."

He covered my mouth with his and his breath caught immediately, picking up on all my feelings, right on the surface. He dove deep, devouring me, and let his hand coast agonizingly slow up my ribs. He stopped and rested it dangerously close before easing himself on his elbow on his other arm and tangling my hair in his hand. Every now and then he would tug and use it to maneuver me, causing me to gasp and groan. That, in turn, would make him groan as he felt what I was feeling. He looked so blissfully happy as he smiled down at me.

I wrapped a leg around the back of his knee and put my hand under his shirt, using that to pull him as close as I could get him. The torture was exquisite. He tugged my hair to give himself access to my neck, his lips finding new places they'd never ventured. Behind my ear, my collarbone, the hollow of my neck.

And then I wasn't in our tent anymore but in a house, on a big bed with the sun peeking through the windows at us. I sat up swiftly, making him lean back a little and almost fall on his butt. He laughed at me as I looked around. I latched my gaze onto the ceiling fan above us, watching it whir and go round, even feeling the wind from it on my face. "How is this real?"

"Devourers have other charms," he murmured and pushed me to lie back down, following me and pressing me into the soft bed. I sighed for more than one reason, but pushed him back.

"So this is real?" I looked around. "This is like really real right now?"

"No, this is really a reverie," he said smugly. "I made this with my mind. I can take you anywhere you want to go, anytime you close your eyes."

"I don't even have to be asleep?"

"No," he said evenly with a little smile. He was enjoying this.

"Why have you never done this to me before?"

"Because we've been a little busy trying to not die," he said with a raised brow. "And I wanted to save it for when you would least expect it. For when it would make you the happiest."

I grinned. "Got any more tricks up your sleeve?"

"Maybe," he grunted into the skin under my chin. "Do you like it?"

"What is this place?"

"This could be our place one day. Maybe." He smiled and looked around. "This is a very human home, isn't it? This is what you would want?"

I stared, stunned silent. "It's beautiful, Enoch. You made this home up…from your imagination?"

"Yeah," he sighed gruffly and let his thumb sweep my jaw line. "Where else would you like to go?"

I felt my eyebrows shoot up. "Where else *can* we go?"

His smiled smugly, sexily. "Anywhere you want to, baby." He leaned his chin on my chest and looked at me. "I'm your genie. Rub me and make your wishes." He smiled wider at my laugh.

"Oh, gosh," I mused. "I haven't been to the beach in—"

I gasped aware on his chest as we laid on a large blanket in the sand.

He chuckled. "I knew you were going to say the beach. So adorably predictable."

I could hear the waves, see the blinding sun and feel the heat of it on my back. I was in a bathing suit—a barely-there little two piece of scraps of material that I was sure Enoch had conjured from the depths of his mind to torture himself into a frenzy. I fingered the strap and looked at him in awe. His grin slid away and he looked a little guilty.

"I was just kidding with the suit. Here."

He moved to sit up and take his shirt off, to give it to me I assumed, but I stopped him, pushing him back down and making him groan with the force of it.

"The suit is fine," I said with an awe-filled chuckle. "I'm yours now, right? And your mine? I'm sure we're going to be seeing…lots of each other."

I even sat up and pulled him with me, peeling the shirt from his body for good measure and tossing it away to prove my point before easing him back down and climbing back over him.

His breath was really loud and rough when it released. He swallowed. "Then what—"

I basically attacked his mouth and felt every feminine bone stand up and clap for joy when his entire body jolted as he coiled around me. He was so strong. He could lift and move me with just his hands. His big, warm palms settled on the backs on my thighs and I thought that would be where he would end his torture, choosing to kiss me and murmur his words there on my lips for the night, but no. He had other plans obviously. With one arm around my waist and the other holding us up, he maneuvered us so that I was now under him. I gasped at the feel of warm sand under me and warm devourer over me. He settled on me and continued his assault wholeheartedly, his lips sucking little places on my neck, his palm sweeping down my thigh and up my side, his chest pressing mine, skin to skin.

"So this is what I have to look forward to," I murmured, my head raised to give him full access to my neck as he kissed the place where my shoulder and neck met. "You taking me anywhere I want to go in the world and making me infinitely happy forever? How is all this really happening to me?" I smiled, but he didn't say anything.

I looked up and he was watching me with a sobered face. He scooted up to be directly over my face and cupped my chin, his finger raking over the hump of my jaw. "Say that again where I can watch your face when you say it."

I smiled slowly and gripped the forearm of the hand that was caressing me. "You make me happy. Is it really that hard to believe?"

"You just said it, sweetheart. How is all this happening to me?" He shook his head, but kept his eyes right on mine. "How the hell do I deserve this?" he whispered.

"We accept the love we think we deserve," I repeated what I'd told him before. "And I'm falling so hard for you, Enoch Thames."

He leaned down and pressed his mouth hungrily to mine before he took both my hands and put them above my head, pressing them to the blanket, and it was there that a decision was made. As he laced my fingers with his, I felt something warm wrap around my chest. I didn't know what to do but trust it. As I looked up into his eyes, I felt his smile in my very soul. I felt the tendrils of my heart reach out for his and hoped that it was what he wanted, too.

He had asked me for forever and now I was asking him for the same thing.

He was kissing me so deep and then he must have felt it, too, because he just stopped moving. His tongue was pressed against mine and then he was pulling away. His eyes looked up and latched onto our entwined hands. Then they were searching my eyes and asking the question. I swallowed and opened my mouth to say something, anything, but he stopped me with a kiss. A kiss that was so soft and thankful, it made me ache.

He ran his hands through my hair and licked his lips as he pulled back. "I can't feel happiness, but if I could, it would feel like this."

One Year Later
Enoch

"All right, kid," I whispered and pointed at the targets placed on the tree line along the bank of the river. The weapons training was taking place and we watched as Aries and Regina practiced with a crossbow. "This is how we do it. You gotta know the ins and outs of every weapon."

"I don't think so."

I turned to find Clara and Fay and grumbled. "Fun's over, little man."

She laughed and shook her head. "I wondered where he went…you know, since he can't walk yet and all."

"You know if he's gone that I've got him," I griped and hoisted him higher in my arms. "Come on, Ben. Can you believe these women?" Ben had been Clara's father's name. There were going to take the name of her parents, whichever it was going to be, boy or girl.

Her laugh got louder as she took him from my arms. He started crying and she laughed even harder.

"See," I told her and held out an arm for Fay to walk into. "Uncle Enoch knows what he's doing."

"Uncle Enoch has let Ben sit in a wet diaper," she scolded with a smile.

"Pssh," I said, brushing the comment off. "Diaper, smiaper. Who needs a clean diaper when there's male bonding going on?" She rolled her eyes and took him away. I yelled. "I'll come rescue you later, buddy!"

I heard Clara's peals of laughter over the sound of the river. I heard it a lot lately. Fay's fingers played with the buttons of my shirt. I covered them with mine and looked down at her.

"One day he'll understand you and be grateful," she said with a smug smile.

"What are you so happy about?" I asked, suddenly intrigued, and put my arms around her, lifting her feet from the ground a little.

"I got off duties for the night, too." She grinned. "So I'm all yours."

"Ooh," I said low. "A drive up the mountain? You and me under the stars? Camping? Alone?"

Her smile left so fast. "Camping? Seriously?"

"But when we're way out there, we can make as much noise as we want."

She slapped my shoulder, but I gripped her tightly as she giggled. "Enoch Thames!"

"I meant singing. I don't want to be embarrassed." I shook my head. "I don't know what you meant—"

"Shut up," she laughed her words and held my face as she kissed me. "I don't care where we go," she whispered and the sincere voice had come out. "I just want to be with you."

I opened my eyes to see her face and there it was, the face that told me she was mine and she loved me despite everything I was.

I smiled. "We're not camping, princess." I ticked my head toward the water and my grin widened. "We will be under the stars though."

She took one look at the boat and I knew I had scored major points. I lifted her dropped jaw with my fingers. "How did you—"

"Franz knows people. It's on loan for the weekend. You saved like…the entire camp. They owe you this one weekend." I leaned in close. "There's a bed under the deck and everything."

She looked at me and her nose brushed my chin. "Like with springs and stuff?"

It was our running joke. It had been *so long* since anyone had slept in a real bed. We stayed in Colorado for two months before we had to leave because winter was coming. We spent some time in New Mexico—keep your friends close and your enemies closer. Since The Wall was there, we thought it might work out to be so close, but that had proved to be hazardous. With Eli and Clara's baby coming, the chance of the wrong person seeing or getting wind of it was just too much, so as soon as we could, we came back to Colorado. They were in the process of getting some type of building that everyone could fit in to keep out the elements. One step at a time.

Fay literally bounced in my arms.

"Go pack," I ordered and swatted her butt.

She saluted and grinned. "Yes, sir."

She took off, the bond wrapped from her to me between us, but turned and ran back to me. She jumped up and wrapped her legs around me.

"Thank you." She kissed me, wrapping her arms tight around my head, like there was no reason on this earth not to. I groaned, feeling the intensity of it hit me. I didn't feel this as often anymore. The bond Fay had given to me that day gave me everything I needed. I never felt starved, ever. I only felt emotion when it was really intense.

And that was fine with me.

She hadn't understood what she was giving me that day. I hadn't told her what the bond did because I never wanted her to bond herself to me for that very reason. I knew she'd do it just because she'd want to make my life easy and I never wanted her to be stuck with me forever. But then I went and mated her to me.

That day on the bank of the river when I held her, her lips blue and lifeless, and thought she was going to die right in front of me—nothing else mattered after that. She was in this. She couldn't escape. The Horde would never let her be. It wasn't like she could run away. She was safest here, with me, with us. I realized that all the reasons why I wanted to keep her away were all the same reasons we should be together.

But when she did bond herself to me, and she hadn't even known what it would mean for me, she had just done it because she truly just wanted me—bloody hell.

When she found out what it meant, she bawled so hard, so happily. She loved to push the envelope though, to *make* me feel her. Like right now, as my fingers dug into her thighs and the tiny groan slipped free, her smug smile curved against my mouth. "You love to torture me," I whispered and smirked.

"I just love you." She sighed and licked her lips. "It's been a year."

I held her tighter. "An amazing year." No jokes. It wasn't funny. It had been a year since she almost died, since she bound me to her, since everything. I put her feet to the ground and brought my hands up, cupping her jaw. "And I love you, too."

She pulled one hand free and laced our hands together on her chest. Our tattooed ring fingers rubbed against each other and I remembered getting them done almost seven months ago. We hadn't gone with traditional wedding rings. This was anything but traditional.

We hadn't done anything crazy. It was just us and the camp. Franz did it for us and the fool grinned through the whole thing. Afterwards, I took her into town, almost a two hour drive through the mountains, and we got these tattoos done. Our bond resembles Clara and Eli's a little, but looks more like vines instead of barb wire. So that's what we got—vines on our ring fingers. Then I took her to a hotel for the night, the only real bed we'd been in for the entire year, except for this weekend.

We spent plenty of time in reveries, but when you woke up in the morning, your back still ached from sleeping on the ground. You could fool your mind, but not your spine. It was nice to get away and take her places, but nothing was like sleeping in an *actual* bed.

Though Eli and Clara had a kid, and were even thinking about having another one down the road, we were not. That was off the table. We were doing everything in our power to prevent it.

More power to them, but it just wasn't the world to bring them into. Besides, we got plenty of playtime with Ben. It was Fay's idea to wipe kids off the table, so I knew she wasn't wanting for it. We were happy. Like, bone-deep happy.

How can you be happy sleeping in a sleeping bag every night in a tent, knowing there were men trying to kill you, always looking over your shoulder waiting for the next attack, knowing that one day war will come, because *it will* come, there is no doubt, and looking at the same faces every day, doing the same thing every day, and still be happy?

She gripped my shirt and pulled me down to kiss me again. "You get a million points for doing this." She kissed me again and brought her knee between mine, rubbing her leg against my knee and thigh to taunt me. My moan had to be heard across the river. "Like a million," she breathed and then smiled so smugly as she turned to walk away. "I'll go pack now."

"You are so gonna get it, princess." I chuckled huskily and watched her behind and legs sway as she walked away.

"Promise?" she threw over her shoulder. I heard her giggle come back to me through the woods.

Yeah. I had never known what happy was before this girl. But even I, a devourer, knew you could be happy like this.

Bone-deep happy.

My name is Enoch Thames and I am a devourer whose life was altered so completely. The one thing I thought I hated most was the one thing that saved me above all else.

The Very End

Playlist

(Theme Song) Monster : Imagine Dragons
Haunt : Bastille
Wanted Man : NeedToBreathe
Fall Into These Arms : New Politics
This : Ed Sheeran
The Baddest Man Alive : Black Keys
Atlas : Coldplay
Shark Attack : Grouplove
Wait : M83
Waiting Alone : Shiny Toy Guns
Laura Palmer : Bastille

Thank you

to the readers who have waited patiently for this story, knowing what I have going on, and still want to be there to read the next book, swoon over the next book boy, fall in love with the next love story. Thank you. You are the reason I do this.

Thank you, Chelsea Fine, for being my sister in that "thing" that we don't speak of. I'm so happy that I got to meet you and I get to text stalk you. It's a privilege. You're the cream to my coffee, the chili to my hotdog. I love your guts, chick.

Thank you, Jamie Magee, for your emails and texts asking where I am and whether Enoch was behaving. It meant a lot. And no, Enoch was never behaving… *wink*

Thank you, Lila Felix, for caring enough to text me when I had doctor visits and even when I didn't. You get me. I <# you.

Thank you, Rachel Higginson. You got me over the book hangover for this book and it was a doozy. You know what I mean. Milkshakes and yards and Hellcat islands. You and me, one day. I love ya, babe. Thank you.

Shelly is a *New York Times & USA Today* Bestselling author from a small town in Georgia and loves everything about the south. She is wife to a fantastical husband and stay at home mom to two boisterous and mischievous boys who keep her on her toes. They currently reside in everywhere USA as they happily travel all over with her husband's job. She loves to spend time with her family, binge on candy corn, go out to eat at new restaurants, buy paperbacks at little bookstores, site see in the new areas they travel to, listen to music everywhere and also LOVES to read.

Her own books happen by accident and she revels in the writing and imagination process. She doesn't go anywhere without her notepad for fear of an idea creeping up and not being able to write it down immediately, even in the middle of the night, where her best ideas are born.

Shelly's website:

www.shellycrane.blogspot.com
https://www.facebook.com/shellycranefanpage
https://twitter.com/AuthShellyCrane

Made in the USA
Middletown, DE
01 December 2023

43796983R00154